# THE SILVER BEAR

# THE
# SILVER
# BEAR

## DEREK HAAS

HODDER &
STOUGHTON

First published in Great Britain in 2008 by Hodder & Stoughton
An Hachette Livre UK company

1

Copyright © Derek Haas 2008

The right of Derek Haas to be identified as the Author
of the Work has been asserted by him in accordance
with the Copyright, Designs and Patents Act 1988

A CIP catalogue record for this title
is available from the British Library

Hardback ISBN 978 0 340 97743 9
Trade Paperback ISBN 978 0 340 97661 6

Printed and bound by Clays Ltd, St Ives plc

Hodder & Stoughton policy is to use papers that are natural, renewable
and recyclable products and made from wood grown in sustainable forests.
The logging and manufacturing processes are expected to conform to
the environmental regulations of the country of origin.

Hodder & Stoughton Ltd
338 Euston Road
London NW1 3BH

www.hodder.co.uk

For Chris, who pulled.
And for Kristi, who pushed.

# THE
# SILVER
# BEAR

# Chapter One

The last day of the cruelest month, and appropriately it rains. Not the spring rain of new life and rebirth, not for me. Death. In my life, always death. I am young; if you saw me on the street, you might think, 'what a nice, clean-cut young man. I'll bet he works in advertising or perhaps a nice accounting firm. I'll bet he's married and is just starting a family. I'll bet his parents raised him well.' But you would be wrong. I am old in a thousand ways. I have seen things and done things that would make you rush instinctively to your child's bedroom and hug him tight to your chest, breathing quick in short bursts like a misfiring engine, and repeat over and over, 'It's okay, baby. It's okay. Everything's okay.'

I am a bad man. I do not have any friends. I do not speak to women or children for longer than is absolutely necessary. I groom myself to blend, like a chameleon darkening its pigment against the side of an oak tree. My hair is cut short, my eyes are hidden behind dark glasses, my dress would inspire a yawn from anyone who passed me in the street. I do not call attention to myself in any way.

I have lived this way for as long as I can remember, although in truth it has only been ten years. The events of my life prior to that day, I have forgotten in all detail, although I do remember the pain. Joy and pain tend to make imprints on memory that do not dim, flecks of senses rather than images that resurrect themselves involuntarily and without warning. I have had precious little of the former and a lifetime of the latter. A week ago, I read a poll that reported ninety percent of people over the age of sixty would choose to be a teenager again if they could. If those same people could have experienced one day of my teenage years, not a single hand would be counted.

The past does not interest me, though it is always there, just below the surface, like dangerous blurs and shapes an ocean swimmer senses in the deep. I am fond of the present. I am in command in the present. I am master of my own destiny in the present. If I choose, I can touch someone, or let someone touch me, but only in the present. Free will is a gift of the present; the only time I can choose to outwit God. The future, your fate, though, belongs to God. If you try to outsmart God in planning your fate, you are in for disappointment. He owns the future, and He loves O. Henry endings.

The present is full of rain and bluster, and I hurry to close the door behind me as I duck into an indiscriminate warehouse alongside the Charles River. It has been a cold April, which many say indicates a long, hot summer approaching, but I do not make predictions. The warehouse is damp, and I can smell mildew, fresh-cut sawdust, and fear.

People do not like to meet with me. Even those whom society considers dangerous are uneasy in my presence. They have heard stories about Singapore, Providence, and Brooklyn. About Washington, Baltimore, and Miami. About London, Bonn, and Dallas. They do not want to say something to make me uncomfortable or angry, and so they choose their words with precision. Fear is a feeling foreign to these types of men, and they do not like the way it settles in their stomach. They get me in and out as fast as they can and with very little negotiation.

Presently, I am to meet with a black man named Archibald Grant. His given name is Cotton Grant, but he didn't like the way 'Cotton' made him sound like a Georgia hillbilly Negro, so he moved to Boston and started calling himself Archibald. He thought it made him sound aristocratic, like he came from prosperity, and he liked the way it sounded on a whore's lips: 'Archibald, slide on over here' in a soft falsetto. He does not know that I know about the name Cotton. In my experience, it is best to know every detail about those with whom you are meeting. A single mention of a surprising detail, a part of his life he thought was buried so deep as to never be found, can cause him to pause just long enough to make a difference. A pause is all I need most of the time.

I walk through a hallway and am stopped at a large door by two towering black behemoths, each with necks the size of my waist. They look at me, and their eyes measure me. Clearly, they were expecting something different after all they've been told. I am used to this. I am used to the disappointment in some of their eyes as they think, 'give me ten minutes in a room with him and we'll see what's shakin'.' But I do not have an ego, and I avoid confrontations.

'You be?' says the one on the right whose slouch makes the handle of his pistol crimp his shirt just enough to let me know it's there.

'Tell Archibald it's *Columbus*.'

He nods, backs through the door, while the other studies me with unintelligent eyes. He coughs and manages, 'You Columbus?' as if in disbelief. Meaning it as a challenge.

I ignore him, not moving a centimetre of my face, my stance, my posture. I am in the present. It is my time, and I own it.

He does not know what to make of this, as he is not used to being ignored, has not been ignored all his life, as big as he is. But somewhere, a voice tells him maybe the stories he heard are true, maybe this Columbus is the badass motherfucker Archibald was talking about yesterday, maybe it'd be best to let the challenge hang out there and fade, the way a radio signal grows faint as a car drives further and further down the highway.

He is relieved when the door opens and I am beckoned into the room.

Archibald is behind a wooden desk; a single light bulb on a wire chain moves like a pendulum over his head. He is not a large man, a sharp contrast from the muscle he keeps around him. Short, well-dressed, with a fire in his eyes that matches the tip of the cigarette stuck in the corner of his mouth. He is used to getting what he wants.

He stands, and we shake hands with a light grip as though neither wants to make a commitment. I am offered the only other chair, and we sit deliberately at the same time.

'I'm a middleman on this,' he says abruptly, so I'll know this from the get-go. The cigarette bobs up and down like a metronome as he speaks.

'I understand.'

'This a single. Eight weeks out, like you say.'

'Where?'

'Outside L.A. At least, that's where this cat'll be at the time.'

Archibald sits back in his chair and folds his hands

on his stomach. He's a businessman, talking business. He likes this role. It makes him think of the business-men behind their desks in Atlanta where he used to go in and change out the trash baskets, replace the garbage with new dark plastic linings.

I nod, only slightly. Archibald takes this as his cue to swivel in his chair and open a file door on the credenza matching his desk. From the cavity, he withdraws a briefcase, and we both know what's inside. He slides it in my direction across the desk and waits.

'Everything you requested's in there, if you want to check it out,' he offers.

'I know where to find you if it's not.'

It's statements like these that can get people into trouble, because they can be interpreted several ways. Perhaps I am making a benign declaration, or pos-sibly a stab at humour, or maybe a little bit of both. But in this business, more often than not, I am making a threat, and nobody likes to be threatened.

He studies my face, his own expression stuck between a smirk and a frown, but whatever he is looking for, he doesn't find it. He has little choice but to laugh it off so his muscle will understand I am not being disrespectful.

'Heh-hah.' Only part of a laugh. 'Yeah. That's good. Well, it's all there.'

I help him out by taking the case off the desk, and

6

he is happy to see me stand. This time, he does not offer his hand.

I walk away from the desk, toward the door, case in hand, but his voice stops me. He can't help himself, his curiosity wins over his cautiousness; he isn't sure if he'll ever see me again, and he has to know.

'Did'ja really pop Corlazzi on that boat?'

You'd be surprised how many times I get this one. Corlazzi was a Chicago underworld luminary responsible for much of the city's butchery in the sixties and seventies, a man who redefined the mafia's role when narcotics started to replace liquor as America's drug of choice. He saw the future first, and deftly rose to prominence. As hated as he was feared, he had a paranoid streak that threatened his sanity. To ensure that he would reign to a ripe old age, he removed himself to a gigantic houseboat docked in the middle of Lake Michigan. It was armed to the teeth, and its only connection with land was through a speedboat manned by his son, Nicolas. Six years ago, he was found dead, a single bullet lodged in the aorta of his heart, though no one heard a shot and the man was behind locked doors with a bevy of guards posted outside.

Now, I don't have to answer this question. I can leave and let Archibald and his entourage wonder how a guy like me could possibly do the things attributed to the name Columbus. This is a tactic I've used in the past, when questions like his are posed. But, today, the last day of the cruelest month, I think differently. I have six eyes on me, and a man's reputation can live for years on the witness of three black guys in a warehouse on the outskirts of Boston.

I spin with a whirl part tornado and part grace, and before an inhale can become an exhale, I have a pistol up and raised in my hand. I squeeze the trigger in the same motion, and the cigarette jumps out of Archibald's mouth and twirls like a baton through the air. The bullet plugs in the brick wall above the credenza as gravity takes the cigarette like a helicopter to a gentle landing on the cement floor. When the six eyes look up, I am gone.

# Chapter Two

Lateral bursts of wind prick the side of my face as I walk into my building. By the time I hear the story again, the scene in Archibald's warehouse will have taken on Herculean proportions. There will have been ten guys, instead of three, all with their guns drawn and trained on me. Archibald will have insulted me by saying, 'There's your case, bitch,' or some other endearment. I will have danced around bullets, mowed down seven guys, and walked on water before the cigarette was shot out of Archibald's mouth. Advertising doesn't hold a candle to the underworld's word of mouth.

My apartment does not reflect the size of my bank account. It is eight hundred square feet, sparsely decorated, with only the furniture and appliances necessary to sustain me for a week, the longest I stay most of the time. I do not have a cleaning service, or take a newspaper, or own a mailbox. My landlord has never met me, but receives a payment for double rent in cash once a year. In return, he asks no questions.

On my one table, I open the case carefully and spread its contents in neat stacks. Twenty dollars to a bill, a hundred bills to a band, five hundred bands in the case. This up front, triple when the job is complete. Underneath all of the money is a manila envelope. The money holds no allure for me. I am as immune to its siren's song as if I had taken a vaccine. The envelope, however, is my addiction.

I slide my finger under the seal and carefully open the flap, withdrawing its contents as though these pages are precious – brittle, breakable, vulnerable. This is what makes my breath catch, my heart spin, my stomach tighten. This is what keeps me looking for the next assignment, and the next, and the next – no matter what the cost to my conscience. This . . . the first look at the person I am going to kill.

Twenty sheets of paper, two binders of photographs, a schedule map, an itinerary, and a copy of a Washington, D.C. driver's license. I savour the first look at these items the way a hungry man savours the smell of steak. This mark will occupy my next eight weeks, and, though he doesn't know it, these papers are the first lines written on his death certificate. The envelope is before me, the contents laid out next to the money on my table, the end of his life now a foregone conclusion, as certain as the rising sun.

Quickly, I hold the first paper to the light that is snaking through my window, my eyes settling on the largest type, the name at the top of the page.

And then a gasp, as though an invisible fist flies through the air and knocks the breath from my lungs.

Can it be? Can someone have known, have somehow discovered my background and set this up as some sort of a joke? But . . . it is unthinkable. No one knows anything about my identity; no fingerprints, no calling card, no trace of my existence ever left carelessly at the scene of a killing. Nothing survives to link Columbus to that infant child taken from his mother's arms by the 'authorities' and rendered a ward of the state.

ABE MANN. The name at the top of the sheet. Can this be a mere coincidence? Doubtful. My experience has proven to me time and time again that coincidence is a staple of fiction, but holds little authority in the real world. I open the binder, and my eyes absorb photograph after photograph. There is no mistake: this is the same Abe Mann who is currently Speaker of the House of Representatives of the United States of America, the same Abe Mann who represents the seventh district of the state of New York, the same Abe Mann who will soon be launching his first bid for his party's nomination for president.

But none of these reasons caused the air to be sucked from my lungs. I have killed powerful men and relish the chance to do so again. There is more to the story of Abe Mann.

Twenty-nine years ago, Abe Mann was a freshman congressman with a comfortable wife and a comfortable house and a comfortable reputation. He attended more sessions of congress than any other congressman, joined three committees and was invited to join three more, and was viewed as a rising star in his party, enjoying his share of air time on the Sunday morning political programmes. He also enjoyed his share of whores.

Abe was a big man. Six-foot-four, and a one-time college basketball star at Syracuse. He married an accountant's daughter, and her frigid upbringing continued unabated to her marriage bed. He stopped loving her before their honeymoon ended, and had his first taste of a prostitute the Monday after they returned from Bermuda. His weekdays he spent at the state capitol as a district representative; his weekends he spent anywhere but home. For five years, he rarely slept in his own bed, and his wife kept her mouth sealed tight, fearful that intimate details of their marriage would end up sandwiched between the world report and the weekend weather on the five o'clock news.

Once elected to serve in the nation's capital, Abe discovered a whole new level of prostitution. There were high-quality whores in New York, mind you, but even they paled in comparison to the women who serviced the leaders of this country. The best part was, he didn't even have to make polite enquiries. He was approached before he was sworn in, approached the first night of his first trip to Washington after the election. A senator, a man he had seen only on television and whom he had never met in person, called him directly at his hotel room and asked if he would like to join him for a party. What an incredible time he had had that night. With the stakes higher, the women so young, so beautiful, and so willing, he had experienced a new ecstasy that still made his mind reel when he thought of it.

Later that year, after he had settled, he grew fond of a hard-bodied black prostitute named Amanda B. Though she argued against it, he forced her to fuck him without a condom, satisfying his growing thirst for bigger and bigger thrills. For about six months, he fucked her in increasingly public locations, in increasingly dangerous positions, with increasingly animalistic ferocity. Each fix begat the next, and he needed stronger doses to satisfy his appetite.

When she became pregnant, his world caved in. He crawled to her in tears, begging for forgiveness. She was not frightened of him until she saw this change. This change meant he was more dangerous than she had anticipated. She knew what would happen next: after the tears, after the self-flagellation, after the 'why me?' and the self-loathing, he would turn. His internal remorse would eventually be directed outward; he would have been made to face his own weakness, and he would not like what he had seen. And so he would destroy that which made him feel helpless. Even in the altered state that cocaine had made of her mind, Amanda B. knew this as surely as she knew anything.

But she liked the way the baby felt inside her. She liked the way it was growing, swelling her stomach, moving inside her. Her! Amanda B., formerly La-Wanda Dickerson of East Providence, Rhode Island, formerly inmate 43254 of the Slawson Home for Girls, her! Amanda B.! *She* could create life as well as any uppity wife of a congressman, any homemaker in a big house on a big lot next to a big lake. Her! As good as any of them.

So she decided to hide. She knew he would come for her, and when he did, she would be gone. She had a friend back home, a john who had proposed to her when she was fourteen. He still called, long distance and not collect either! He would take her in, would hide her from the congressman when he came looking. If she could just get to him . . .

But she didn't make it to Rhode Island. Instead, she ended up in the hospital, her nose bleeding, her lungs exploding, her heart beating holes into her chest. The police had found her seven-months-pregnant frame in the basement of an abandoned tenement building during a routine drug raid, a rubber cord tied around her bicep, a needle sticking out of her forearm. She was checked into the hospital as Jane Doe number 13 that day. The next day, she went into labour and gave birth to a four-pound boy. Social Services took him from her before she had held him for more than a minute.

Congressman Mann saw her for the last time two months later. Having seen the error of his ways, having rededicated his life to his country, his wife, and his God, he had her forcibly escorted from his front yard as she screamed louder and with more vehemence than she had ever screamed in her life. Ten days after the police report was filed, she was found dead in an alley behind a Sohio gas station, a knife handle sticking at an awkward angle from her neck. The policeman on the scene, a sixteen-year veteran named William Handley, speculated the wound was self-inflicted, though the coroner thought the circumstances of the death were inconclusive.

It took me two and a half years to put all that together. I did not ask the clay's question of who is the potter until I had achieved adulthood, not believing I would survive long enough to care. Then, after killing my eighth mark in three years, achieving a level of professionalism few have matched, I started to wonder who I was. Where did I come from? Who could possibly have sired me? The past, for which I had held no deference, reached out its huge, black paw and batted me right in the face.

So I clawed and scratched and exercised the necessary patience and restraint, and slowly put the jigsaw puzzle together, starting with the edges and working my way toward the centre. A newspaper story connected to a hospital report connected to a police record until it all took shape and became whole. Once the puzzle was complete, I decided to dismiss the past once and for all. The present would be my domain, always the present. Every time I had tried to befriend the past, it chose to have no amity for me. Well, no more. I would bury my mother, Amanda B., so deep I would never find her again. And so I would my father, Congressman Abe Mann of New York.

And then, here is his name at the top of the sheet. Seven black letters printed in a careful hand, strong in their order, powerful in their conciseness. ABE MANN. My father. The next person I am to kill, in Los Angeles, eight weeks from now.

Can this be a coincidence, or has someone discovered my secret past and put the jigsaw puzzle together as I had? In my line of work, I can take no chances with the answer. I have to react quickly, waste as little time as possible, for if this does prove to be just another assignment, I'll have to compensate for each minute missed.

I, too, have a middleman. Pooley is the closest thing to friend or family I have, but we prefer the noncommittal label 'business associates'. I take one more glance over the documents, stack everything back in the case, and head out the door.

A hotel a block away provides me with quick access to taxicabs whenever I need them. The rain diminishing, I make my way over to where the hotel's doorman can hail me a car. The driver feels like chatting me up, but I stare out the window and let the buildings slide by outside like they're on a conveyer belt, one after the other, each looking just like the one before it. Stymied, the driver lights a cigarette and turns up the radio, a daygame, a businessman's special, broadcasting from Fenway.

We make it to Downey Street in SoBo, and I have the driver pull over to a nondescript corner. I do nothing that will cause him to remember me; I pay a fair tip and move up the street quickly. A day from now, he won't be able to distinguish me from any other fare.

I buy two coffees from a Greek delicatessen and climb the stoop to a loft apartment above the neighbouring bakery. I am buzzed in before I can even juggle the styrofoam cups and press the button. Pooley must be at his desk.

'You brought me coffee?' He acts surprised as I hand him one of the cups and sit heavily in the only other chair in the room. 'You thoughtful bastard.'

'Yeah, I'm going soft.'

I hoist the case onto his desk and slide it over to him.

'Archibald's?'

'Yep,' I answer.

'He give you any problems?'

'Naah, he's all bluster. What I want to know is: who's he working for?'

This catches Pooley off guard. Ours is a business where certain questions aren't asked. The less you know – the fewer people you know, I should say – the better your chances of survival. Middlemen are as common as paper and ink, another office supply, a necessity to conduct business. They are used for a reason: to protect us from each other. Everyone understands this. Everyone respects this. You do not go asking questions, or you end up dead or relocated or physically unable to do your job. But those seven letters at the top of the page changed the rules.

'What?' he asks. Maybe he hadn't heard me right. I can't blame him for hoping.

'I want to know who hired Archibald to work as his go-between.'

'Columbus,' Pooley stammers. 'Are you serious?'

'I'm as serious as you've ever known me.'

This is no small statement, and Pooley knows it. We go back nearly twenty years, and he's seen me serious all my life. This breach of professional etiquette has him jumpy. I can see it on his face. Pooley is not good at hiding his emotions, not ever.

'Goddammit, Columbus. Why're you asking me that?'

'Open the case,' I say.

He looks at it suspiciously now, as if it can rise off the table and bite him, and then back at me. I nod without changing my expression, and he spins the case around and unhinges the snaps.

'In the envelope,' I urge when he doesn't see anything looking particularly troublesome.

He withdraws the envelope and slides his finger under the flap as I did. When he sees the name at the top of the page, his face flushes.

'You gotta be shitting me.'

Like I said, Pooley is practically my brother, and as such, is the only one who knows the truth about my genesis. When I was thirteen and he was eleven, we were placed with the same foster family, my sixth in five years, Pooley's third. By then, I could take whatever shit was thrown my way, but Pooley was still a boy, and he had been set up pretty well in his last home. He had an old lady for a foster mother, and the worst thing she did was to make him clean the sheets when she shit the bed. Not a particularly easy job for a nine-year-old, but nothing compared to what he had to survive at the Cox house after the old lady passed away.

Pete Cox was an English professor at one of the fancy schools outside Boston. He was a deacon at his church, a patron at the corner barbershop, and an amateur actor at the neighbourhood theatre. His wife had suffered severe brain damage four years prior to our arrival. She had been in the passenger seat of a Nissan pickup truck when the driver lost control of the wheel and rolled the truck eleven times before it came to rest in a field outside Framingham.

The driver was not her husband. The last person who could substantiate their whereabouts was the clerk at the Marriott Courtyard Suites . . . when they checked out . . . together.

Subsequently, his wife occupied a hospital bed in the upstairs office of Pete's two-storey home. She was heavily medicated, never spoke, ate through a tube, and kept on living. Her doctors thought she might live another fifty years, if properly cared for. There was nothing wrong with her body, just her brain, jammed in by the door handle when it broke through her skull.

Pete decided to take in foster children, since he would never have children of his own. His colleagues felt he was a brave man, a stoic; they certainly would have understood if he had divorced his wife after the circumstances of the accident came to light. But not our Pete. No, our Pete felt as though his wife's condition was a consequence of his own sin. And as long as he took care of his wife, as long as he showed God he could handle that burden, then it was okay if his sin continued. And grew. And worsened.

Pete liked to hurt little boys. He had been hurting little boys on and off since he was eighteen. 'Hurting them' could mean a number of things, and Pete had tried them all. He had nearly been caught when he was first learning his hobby after he had sliced off the nipple of an eight-year-old who was selling magazine subscriptions door-to-door. Pete caught up with him in the alley behind his cousin's apartment – just luck he had been visiting at the time! – and invited the kid to show him his sales brochure. With the promise of seventeen subscription purchases, which would qualify the kid for a free Sony Walkman and make him the number-one salesman in his Cub Scout den, Pete got him to step behind a dumpster and take off his shirt. He had the nipple off in no time, but he hadn't anticipated the volume of the child's scream. It was so loud, so visceral, so animal, it excited Pete like a drug; yet, at the same time, windows were going up all over the block. Pete booked it out of there, and no one ever came looking for him. He promised himself to be more discreet the next time. And the next time. And the next.

By the time we came to live with him, Pete had hurt hundreds of children all over the country. He had thought his wife to be his saviour, the only woman who had really, truly cared for him, and for a while after they were married, he had stopped doing what he did to little boys. But an addiction is tough to put away permanently; it sits in dark recesses, gathering strength, biding its time until it can unleash itself, virgin and hungry, again. It was a week after Pete had fallen off the wagon, had done an unmentionable thing to a nine-year-old, when his wife had had her accident. How could he not blame himself for her fate? The Bible spends a great deal of time explaining the 'wages' of sin, and what were his wife's infidelity and her crumpled brain but manifestations of the evil he had committed on that boy? So he took care of her, and four years later, signed up with the state to be a foster parent.

I don't need to shock you with the atrocities Pooley and I endured in the two years we lived in the Cox house. Rather, to understand the relationship we now share, I'll tell you about the last night, the night before we were sent to finish out our youth at Juvenile upstate.

I was fifteen then, and had figured out ways to make my body stronger, despite Cox's best efforts to keep us physically emaciated. When he went to work, I put chairs together and practised push-ups, my legs suspended between them. I moved clothes off the bar in the closet and pulled myself up – first ten times, then twenty, then hundreds. I bench-pressed the sofa, I ran sprints in the hallway, I squatted with the bookcase on my back. All of this while Pete was gone; everything put back and in its place before he returned. I tried to get Pooley to work his body with me, but he was too weak. He wanted to, I could tell, but his mind wouldn't let him see the light at the end of the tunnel, so much had been taken out of him.

On this day, the last day, Pete had given his students a walk. He had not felt good, had started to come down with something, and when the dean of the department told him to go on home and rest, Pete decided to take his advice before he changed his mind. This is why he entered his house not at four o'clock like he usually did, but at two-fifteen. This is why he found me surrounded by books all over the floor, the bookcase lofted on my back, my taut body in mid-squat.

'What the fuck?' was all he could muster, before his eyes narrowed and he came marching toward me.

I tossed the bookcase off my back like I was bucking a saddle, and looked for the easiest escape route, but there wasn't one, and before I could move, his arms were around me. He hoisted me off the ground – I couldn't have weighed more than a hundred and twenty pounds – and threw me head-first into the wall. Instead of cracking, my head ripped through the plaster into a wooden beam. Dazed, I pushed away as fast as I could, shaking wall dust from my hair, but he was on me again, and this time, he held me up in a bear hug. His face was both angry and ecstatic, and he squeezed until I couldn't breathe and my eyes went bleary with tears. I think he would have killed me. I was getting too old to bully and he knew I was building up resistance. It would have been safer to kill me. To go ahead and finish this here and now. He still had one more little boy he could torture.

23

From up the stairs, Pooley found his voice. 'Let go of him, you stupid motherfucker!'

This got our attention, both of us, and distracted Cox enough to make him drop me. From *my* mouth, he was used to hearing such language, such resentment, such fury, but not from little Pooley. We both jerked our heads simultaneously and looked up the stairs.

The door guarding Mrs Cox stood open. The padlock that usually kept it firmly closed was somehow forced, wood scrapings cutting claw scratches into the wall. Pooley stood just outside the door, his tiny body shaking, drenched with sweat, a glass shard in his hand, blood dripping from the end in large red drops.

Pete's face metamorphosed so dramatically, it was like someone had flipped a switch, turning from acid rage to sudden confusion and trepidation. 'What'd you do?' was all he could manage, and his knees actually wobbled.

Pooley didn't answer; he just stood there, trembling, his face strained, blood and sweat mingling on the carpet at his feet.

'What'd you do?' Pete shouted a second time, his voice marked with desperation. Again, Pooley didn't answer.

Pete launched for the stairs and ascended them in five quick steps. I was close behind, prepared to tackle him with everything I had if he went for Pooley. But

24

he didn't. He took two more steps toward his wife's open door, peeked into the room fearfully, as though hands might suddenly reach out and grab him, and then collapsed inside.

I got to Pooley as tormented wails began to waft from the open door. 'Come on,' I said.

Pooley's eyes continued to stare off into space.

'Let's get out of here,' I added. The urgency in my voice snapped some life back into his face and his eyes settled on me.

'I had to,' he said weakly.

'I know,' I offered.

I put my hand on his arm, and he let the shard drop to the floor. The blood caught it, and it landed sideways, red flecks marring the beauty of the glass. We stepped over it and walked down the stairs. I picked up the bookcase again and heaved it into the living room window, somehow knowing instinctively the front door had been double bolted before Pete turned and found me there.

We climbed out of the window and tasted the air outside for the first time in over a year, just as the loudest wail rose from the dark upstairs. 'I'm sorry! I'm so sorry! I'm so sorry!'

All those months Pooley had been silent, pretending to be resigned inside himself, he had really been watching, studying, understanding the motivations of our Pete. Taking his beatings in silence, letting me take mine, but watching, waiting. Twice he had overheard Pete in Mrs Cox's room, pouring out his penitence to her mindless eyes. Twice he had heard Pete begging for forgiveness, only to increase his savagery two hours later. So Pooley began to figure out that Pete needed her there to continue doing what he did to us. He needed someone who wouldn't judge him, but would sit passively and let him forgive himself so he could do it again. While I trained, trying to make my body stronger so I could one day fight back, Pooley cracked a mirror in the back bathroom, sharpened a shard on the side of the bedroom head-board, and waited. When Pete came home early and found me getting stronger, he knew he could wait no longer.

The police picked us up before we had gone a mile. We were indicted for killing Mrs Cox, and my descriptions of our treatment seemed to fall on deaf ears. I had a petty-crime juvenile record in my past, and Pooley was done talking to adults for a long time. I can't say I blamed him; he saved my life, after all. Nor was I surprised when we were convicted. But because of some of the oddities that came out of Pete's mouth when he talked cryptically to the judge about swift, painful discipline – lending some credence to what I had said about our treatment – we were tried as juveniles and sent upstate to finish out our youth.

★　　★　　★

So Pooley was the first assassin I had known. When I decided to begin this life professionally – or you might say it was decided for me – he was a natural to be my middleman, though he wasn't my first.

# Chapter Three

Pooley agrees the coincidence surrounding my father is too odd to let pass without some digging. Since I need to head west without delay, he'll handle the shovel for me. We agree to speak again when I call next week from the road.

My rule is eight weeks out. I will not agree to complete a job in less than that time, and, as such, have turned down quite a few assignments, even when offers for more money have been dangled like grapes. I can flawlessly plan and execute a job in less time; of that, I have no doubt. But assassinating a target takes psychological preparation, and short-changing yourself in that area can lead to debilitation long after the mark is in the grave.

I open the folder again and this time, study the contents without flinching. He will be travelling by bus, a 'whistle-stop' tour crisscrossing the country, culminating in Los Angeles at the Democratic National Convention. His path is strategically haphazard, planned randomness, with stops in most of the major television markets surrounding battleground states and enough small towns peppered in so that no economic demographic will feel slighted. Three thousand miles and a million handshakes in eight weeks. I will follow the same route, and will wait for him in the Midwest, allowing him to catch up, before I follow him the rest of the way to California.

The next morning, a rental car is parked out on my street with no paperwork to sign, no instructions to receive, the keys on the floorboard under the steering column. A beige car, a sedan, with nothing to distinguish it from the millions of other cars sprawling across American highways at any given time. With only a small duffel tossed in the back seat and a larger case lodged in the trunk, I head west, the sun at my back.

When I pull over to eat lunch at a small roadside dinette with the provocative name SUE'S NO. 2, I am approached by a prostitute. I had grabbed a booth in the back of the restaurant in order to avoid contact with the local denizens of this somewhere-town, but this girl could care less where I sat. She homed in on me as soon as the bells jingled on the door.

She is dressed in a skirt that stops well above her knees and a white halter that exposes the baby fat around her middle. Her hair is stringy blond with burgundy roots and hangs away from her head like a web. She possesses a crooked nose but an uncommonly pretty mouth with perfectly straight teeth. Her eyes are sharp and intelligent.

'Hey there, mon frer,' she says, plopping down in the seat across from me. My guess is she cannot weigh more than a hundred pounds nor be older than seventeen.

I don't say anything, and she proceeds, unfazed.

'Here's what I'm thinking. I got dropped off in this shithole town, and I need a lift outta here.' This comes out between smacks of bright purple gum and the smell of grapes left too long on the vine. 'So I'm prepared to grant you favours in exchange for a lift.'

'A lift where?'

'Wherever it is you're headed.'

'What kind of favours?'

She drops her chin and looks at me from the tops of her eyes like I don't have the sense God gave me. Just then, the waitress approaches. The girl waits for me to order, and before the waitress can disappear, I find myself asking her if she's hungry.

'Fuckin' starvin', man.'

The waitress takes an order for steak and eggs and hashbrowns and bacon if they have any left over from breakfast. Oh, and some orange juice and some milk and that'll be it. The girl's eyes are merry now; there is a break in the storm clouds. I don't normally talk to people, but it's been an abnormal week and those merry eyes stir something inside me I thought wasn't there.

'How'd you get here?'

'This nut-rubber wanted some company for his ride over to Boston. He wanted me to jerk him along the way.' Hand gestures for emphasis. 'I gave him what he asked for and when we pulled over here to get something to eat, he split as soon as I stepped out of the car.' Matter-of-factly, as though she were telling me about her day at school. 'Stiffed me, too, the bastard. It's gettin' to where there's not any honest people around.'

'How old are you?'

'I lost track.'

I swear she's seventeen. 'What's the last age you remember being?'

'Let's not talk about me. Let's talk about—'

But she's interrupted by the food. We both eat in silence; I because I enjoy it, she because she can't get the breakfast into her mouth fast enough. The food is flying up to her face like a power shovel at full steam, and she is as unembarrassed as a hog at a trough. She devours all of hers, and when I proffer half of my plate, she attacks it.

After I've left money for the tab, she asks, 'So how about that ride?'

'What do you think?'

Smiling now with those beautiful ivory teeth, she

puts one finger in her mouth. 'I think I've got a pretty good shot at taggin' along with you.'

She's asleep in the passenger seat, and I am pissed. Pissed I let my guard down, pissed I've committed a cardinal sin, pissed I've ignored every professional instinct in my ken to allow her to share this car with me. I can still kill her, can still pull the car down one of these farm-to-market roads, roll the tires against some deserted brush, and pop, pop, dump the body where it won't be found for weeks. She won't be missed, that's certain. Except, goddammit, people saw us at the diner, the waitress, the old man in coveralls at the counter, the couple in the booth at the far end of the joint. They saw her lock in on me, and they saw us leave together, and they saw us get into my beige sedan. People noticed. They noticed, goddammit. What is happening to me?

Bad luck. The name at the top of the page was bad luck, and now picking up this girl-whore is as black bad as it can get. My stomach is queasy with the blackness. I must be slipping.

'So, where are we headed?' She puts her bare feet up on the dashboard in front of her and blinks groggily.

'Philadelphia.'

'Yeah? Good. That's where I came from.'

'Originally?'

'Naah,' she snorts, finding the question funny. 'Originally I'm from a little hovel outside of Pittsburgh that you've never heard of. Recently, I'm from Philly.'

'That's where you . . . work?'

She snorts again, not at all self-conscious about the way it makes her sound like a sow. 'Yeah, work. Working girl.' She pauses thoughtfully, and then, as though she's struggling with the weight of her question, 'What do you think about that?'

'About what you do?'

'Yeah. I'm curious. You seem like a normal dude. What's a normal dude think about a working girl?'

'I think it can't be too good of a way to make a living.'

'You got that right, buddy. You certainly got that right.'

'So, why do it, then?'

'I don't know. I can tell you one thing, I'm rarely lucid enough to sit and think about it. You got any liquor in here?' She tries to swivel in her seat to look in the back, but when she reaches for my duffel, I grab her with my free hand and spin her around hard.

'Owww. Shit, man! I'm just looking to see if you got anything to drink!'

'I don't.'

'Well you don't have to be a cocksucker about it.' She's showing me the same mouth that can use words like 'hovel' and 'lucid' can spew vitriol as well. And she's testing the envelope to see how far she can push

34

it. Was the way I spun her around portentous of a beating to come? Did she get a rise out of me with the severity of the way she pronounced cocksucker, the way she paused right before the word, collecting her breath and then pounding that first syllable like she hit it with a hammer? COCKsucker! We drive on in silence. I can tell she'd rather pass the time talking than pouting, but she wants me to make the first move.

After two minutes, she gives up. 'I was just looking to see if you had something to drink.'

'I don't.'

She decides to get off the subject. 'You like music?'

'I like silence.'

This seems to do the trick, and for a few minutes more, the only sound in the car is her nasal breathing, in and out, in and out, like wind through a cracked window.

'I need to pee,' she says suddenly, nodding at the approaching exit where a Texaco sign pokes just above the tree line.

I throw up my blinker and guide the car toward the exit. As we approach, I can't help but notice a farm road running directly behind the service station, leading off into obscurity. Maybe I can get away with it, with a little extra time. If I can find some soft earth, I can dig a little hole to hide her body, and it'll be months, maybe years before anyone finds the remains. But it's broad daylight and I don't know this

35

road and any dumb farmer could happen along at just the right time.

By the time I've rejected the temptation, she's opened the door. I watch her ask the attendant where the restrooms are and he hands her a giant block of wood with a key attached and points around to the back of the building. I watch him watch her all the way out the door, and when he catches me observing him, he quickly looks back down at the binder he had splayed on the counter.

What am I doing here? I should just gun the car and forget I ever saw this girl, but for some reason, I'm paralyzed. What is it about those teeth and that mouth? What do I see in them?

I turn off the ignition and head into the convenience store portion of the station where the clerk gives me a once-over and shuffles his binder down below the counter. I move to the drinks stacked like bricks up to the ceiling in the back of the store and withdraw a six-pack of Budweiser. For someone whose every move is performed to draw the least amount of attention – domestic over import in rural Pennsylvania – I realize I've already attracted notice just by parking the car and having this girl ask for the bathroom key. The clerk's once-over wasn't because he was worried I'd shoplift something from the store; he wanted to know what kind of man would pick up a girl like that. And he is going to remember who it was and what the man looked like when and if he is asked.

This is how it happens. In the game I play, you cannot give in to temptation, even if temptation is merely to hold a conversation with someone, to connect with another human being on a superficial level. And once you give in to temptation, even if you only do it one time, then the dominoes start to topple until the entire floor is covered with a dark blanket.

I pay for the beer and the clerk only grunts at me without meeting my eyes when he hands over the change. Maybe this isn't so bad. I've done a thoughtful thing for this girl, and the clerk is back looking at his binder before I even leave the store. Maybe I can pull this off, talk to this girl, gain some insight into her world and what she imagined she would be doing with her life. Find out where her life took the left turn instead of the right, where she missed the exit and eventually got lost and discovered that her map was terribly inaccurate. Maybe I can learn about someone for once, someone whose life had been like my mother's, with no hidden motives.

In the car, I slide back behind the wheel and put the six-pack on the seat so the girl will see it when she returns. It's as simple as that, buying her breakfast, giving her this six-pack of beer, and that smile will come to her lips again, and she will lean back in her seat, and she will be warm and rosy, and she won't have to say things like cocksucker and pee and we can have a normal conversation like normal people.

37

A moment exists in time – a flash of a moment – right before you realize how fucked you are. You can't explain it scientifically, but a shiver settles on the back of your neck as though someone placed an ice cube there. The fine hairs on your neck stand erect like they've been jolted with electricity. A rush of heat flashes through your body and your muscles all contract in unison. This happens instantaneously, when your mind hasn't quite caught up to your body's impulse. It is what I felt when I happened to glance in the back seat.

My duffel. She had reached for my duffel and I had immediately seized her arm and jerked her around hard. Therefore, there must be something valuable in the duffel. She must have taken it while I was in the store.

I bolt from the car and around to the bathroom, knowing instinctively the clerk's eyes are riveted on me. Nothing. Just a key stuck in the open door of a filthy bathroom and no trace of the girl or my bag. Behind the Texaco, a thick growth of trees, a country road leading to oblivion, and no sign of the fucking girl. Pandora has climbed out of her box.

My breath escapes quickly, four quick bursts, and then I'm off into the woods. I don't even know what goddamn name to call her, to call out, so I just stay quiet, a determined expression now blanching my face. I have to improvise, to hunt her quickly. How long will the clerk look at that rental car parked in front of the store before he calls the police with a declaration that something a little strange is going on down at the Texaco? He saw the girl. He saw me. He saw her go around to the back and then he saw me spring from the car after her. Had I even shut the door of the car? I'm not sure. Son-of-a-bitch, how had I let this get so out of hand?

I have five minutes, maybe ten to find her before the clerk ventures out to see if we're in the bathroom together. After that, who knows? Another five minutes to call the police? I'm fucked. That's all there is to it.

Trees everywhere, and then, a clearing, and I catch a glimpse of her just as she crosses into the growth about a tenth of a mile from where I stand. She caught sight of me, too, and I spot a panic in her face usually reserved for wild prey. Maybe she's seen what's in the bag and she's spooked. But she hasn't dropped the duffel either; I can see its yellow flash caught against her dark skirt.

I close the distance in no time. She's skittish, and she makes a mistake, turns and trips over a dead oak stump. Her hands go up as my footsteps crunch through the dead leaves, on her back, arms bent, scrambling, scratching the air, trying to get me off before I'm even there.

And then my foot comes down on her neck, twisting her face into the dirt so that those pretty teeth are smeared with earth.

'No, mister. Please. I don't want it. I didn't mean to . . . I didn't mean . . . I didn't mean . . .'

Fighting with everything she has, every inch of strength she can muster, her arms wailing at my shin, beating my pants leg, her eyes desperate with fear.

And then I step down harder until I hear the bones in her neck crack like wood.

The forest is silent in the peculiar way nature seems to go mute when a living creature is killed. I hesitate to say 'innocent' creature, because if she hadn't been so stupid, if she hadn't been so goddamn reckless, she'd still be alive and we'd be chatting on our way to Philadelphia, making a connection, talking about the normal things normal people talk about and her mouth would be smiling and sipping on a beer rather than silent and gaping and half-filled with muck, and leaves, and decay.

Or maybe the woods aren't silent at all. Maybe my ears are ringing so loudly all other sounds are drowned out. I am breathing hard and a bead of sweat has rolled from my eyebrows to the tip of my nose, but the silence is implacable, as thick as cream. Underneath my boot, the girl remains still, her energy as used up and wasted as her life.

I will need a little luck. I prop the girl on my shoulders as though I'm carrying a wounded soldier, and hurry back through the woods toward the convenience store. A little luck, a little luck. That's all I'm asking. My footsteps are firm, finding solid ground again and again, weaving in and out of the trees, the back of the store looming larger and larger through the brush. Her weight is slight, and her body bobs up and down on my shoulders, light as a backpack. Thirty feet, twenty, and no sign of the clerk. Just stay at your counter, friend. Keep marking in your binder, counting up that inventory, and you'll soon forget about us, just another couple of customers amidst a constant string of travellers.

I break through the tree line and I'm back at the store, the block of wood still dangling from the doorknob like a pendulum. In a quick step, I'm in the room with the body on my back and the block of wood in my hand and the door shut tight. Almost there. Stay with me, luck.

The smell in the bathroom is horrible, and stains splotch the walls like a foul mosaic. It doesn't take me long to work myself up. The stench, the agitation, the degradation of killing in this animalistic manner, her body propped across the sink, her head facing me, her lips curling back away from her teeth in a sneer that is accusatory and mocking and hopeless. I double over and retch until I can feel the pulse thick in my ears.

He knocks as I finish my second heave.

'Are you okay in there?'

Luck is a funny thing. I open the door, carrying the girl in my arms, quickly, out into the open. 'Do you have a hose?' I say, and his eyes immediately go over my shoulder to the bathroom, his nose curling.

'Awww, shit.'

'Sorry, man. She got sick.' I smooth the girl's hair with my supporting hand.

He doesn't even look at us, shaking his head. 'Don't worry about it,' he says, resigned, and passes me to survey the mess in the stall.

I don't wait for him to give us a second look. I am around the building and into the car before he can even hook up the hose, my bag and the whore's body laid to rest in the wide back seat.

# Chapter Four

I wash myself the best I can at a highway rest stop. I buried the body a hundred yards inside a thick growth of trees off of a deserted farm-to-market road with nothing but a tyre iron and my bare hands. It was a messy operation. Messy because I don't know the land, don't have time to do it the right way, don't have time to plant the body deep enough so it won't be found for decades. And yet I am not worried. If a hiker or the landowner stumbles upon her corpse, I did take the few minutes necessary to make it difficult to identify.

I am still blanketed in dirt when I enter the brick courtyard of the Rittenhouse Hotel. I pass through the lounge, only slowing for a hasty check-in, and then up to my room, fending off assistance with my bags from duelling bellboys. Just get me to my room, get me to a shower, let me wash off the grime and the smell of this day gone sour.

The room is enormous, with a large window over-looking Rittenhouse Square and the city. More furniture stands in this room than I've owned in my entire life. I would not choose to live this way, but this is where Abe Mann will be staying in a few weeks, and I need to forget who I am and get my mind right. For the first time on this job, I will get my mind right.

To hunt a human being, it is not enough to plot from afar, externally. An assassin must understand his prey by storming the target's mind the way an army storms enemy territory. He must live, sleep, eat, breathe as the target does, until he has merged with the target, until they are one. To kill a man, he must become the man, so that he can live as himself beyond the man.

The water is a blessing, as purifying as a baptism. Just relax, relax, re-lax, and this day, and everything in it, will be just like the soap washing down the drain. Gone and forgotten.

But no. The girl hides right behind my eyes, popping out like a child playing peek-a-boo whenever I close the lids. I've killed people without blinking, without feeling a twinge of remorse, and yet this girl continues to haunt me like an itch under a plaster cast.

'That's right,' she says. 'You and me. We're stuck together. Scratch-scratch.'

I shake my head, and the water in my hair sprays the shower curtain. But I do not open my eyes. I like the way she looks. I actually like looking at her, I giggle to myself. And then for the first time, I think my past has finally caught me, my defenses are being stormed by a battering-ram of life I've tried so desperately to shake. I thought if I ran fast enough, if I shirked the past off my back the way I bucked that bookcase in Mr Cox's living room, it would be too heavy and slow to catch me. But it's here, in this shower, in full force, pissed off and angry and bringing madness along for the ride.

'Tell me about your mother,' the girl says, so close to my face I can smell the dirt in her breath.

'What's that supposed to mean?' I mumble, although I can't be sure if it's aloud or in my head.

'I want to understand,' she says, floating, swimming, just on the other side of my eyes. 'Tell me about your girl. Tell me about Jake.'

Then the water runs hot, a surge of searing heat, and the spell is broken. I jump back from the stream and wait for it to cool a little. Finally, it tapers back to a nice tepid temperature, and I rinse quickly, towel off, and collapse on top of the bed. I feel my eyes close, searching for the dead girl.

I did have a girl once. For just a few months, a long time ago. She had honey-blond, shoulder-length hair and a chocolate lab named Bandit. She had bright, cheerful eyes that were amplified behind thick black glasses and a single-bedroom apartment above a bookstore in Cambridge. She was smart, engaging, lithe, and alive. Her name was Jake.

We met after my release from Waxham Juvenile Corrections and right before my new term started, the bondage that began when I shook hands with a fat man named Vespucci. The handshake with that dark Italian ended things forever, but before that, right before that, was the only period in my life where I felt normal. The only period where I believed, if only for a few fleeting months, I could make it, could whip life, could become a 'new' man, like the priest, Father Steve, always repeated at Waxham.

'You came in here dirty, debased boys, but you can leave here as new men. The blessed waters of for-giveness will cleanse you, make you new men, but only if you bathe in a pool of repentance.' And I wanted to believe it, every word. For someone who had been a dirty, debased boy all his life, who didn't know his mother or father, I thirsted to be a new man the way a desert traveller thirsts for just one drink of water. For once, just one time, I wanted to be a new man drinking a clean glass of water.

When I was released, I hurried to Boston, where Father Steve secured me a job loading cases of beer into trucks. Apparently, Father Steve's brother hadn't received the same telegram from God that had found Steve, and he had prospered as a beer distributor. The siblings were cut from the same cloth, though, and Father Steve's brother helped 'new men' get on their feet, get closer to that cool glass of water, even if lugging stacks of beer was the only way he knew to get them there.

A couple of weeks after taking the job, I received the first paycheck of my life. Me, orphan, foster child, ex-convict, me, with a cheque for four hundred and seventy-two dollars made out in my name. I wrote to Pooley as soon as I got home. We were sentenced to serve until we were eighteen, and since I was older, I had gotten out a couple of years before him. Receiving a letter was one of the few joys a boy could have at Waxham, so I sent him one just about every day. He had to know I had made it, there was something to look forward to, something to dream about in the darkness of that damn rat cage. He had to know I had received a paycheck, was opening a savings account, was waiting for him when he got his release.

It was on the way to the bank to cash my new cheque that I met her. I didn't know how to open an account, but Father Steve's brother had explained to me how easy it was, how glad the banks would be to hold my money each week. I was wearing a clean shirt, and my pants were only slightly dirty. I felt good.

She grabbed me by the shoulder and spun me around. 'Louis?' she had said. My instinct was to watch out, to protect myself, so seldom had I let someone touch me. But for some reason, as firm as her grip had been on my shoulder, I didn't feel threatened.

47

'Oh, I'm sorry,' she said. 'I'm so sorry, I thought you were my brother.'

I felt a smile coming. Her laughter was real, exposed, infectious. 'I'm sorry,' she finally finished, catching her breath, and then her hand extended toward me. 'From the side, you looked exactly like my brother. I'm Jake.'

'Jake?'

'Jacqueline. Jake. I like Jake better.'

I nodded, grinning like a madman, and shook her hand. Damn, did it feel soft. 'I do too.'

Her eyes narrowed, still smiling, and she examined me almost with affection. 'I swear. From the side, I thought Lou had come to town.'

'Yeah?'

'It was uncanny. I was just heading in to have a coffee, and bam, there goes Lou, walking right past me.'

'Except it was me.'

'Yep. From the side, the spitting image. Man, that's something.'

The way she said 'something' – she sort of lifted up on her toes and then rocked back on her heels – I melted like candle wax.

'Say, you want to go in and have that coffee with me?'

Somehow, I found my voice. 'Yeah. I'd like to.'

I'd never had coffee in my life.

★   ★   ★

Every day for a week, we met at the frog pond and watched the tourists take their shoes off and wade in the ankle-high water. She talked a lot, and I loved to hear her husky voice tickle my ears like a feather. God, that girl could talk, and I would have done anything to stay there, my head in her lap, watching the tourists pass by.

'My philosophy is this. We don't owe anything to our family, to our parents, just for conceiving us and putting a roof over our heads for so many years. The question becomes, do you like these people? Do you want to spend time with them, have a coffee with them, eat dinner with them? If the answer is "no", then so be it. Why should you waste your time with them if you don't even like their company? What society deems appropriate is contrary to rudimentary truths. Life is precious. Life is fleeting. Life is fragmentary. It's here today and *whip!* it's gone before you know it. One second you're a little girl asking if you can please, please, please get the Barbie easy-bake oven for Christmas and the next minute you're twenty-one and you have nothing in common with these people you call mom and dad. They don't understand anything about you. You are speaking a foreign language to them. So why do you care about them at all?'

I just stared up at her chin as it bobbed up and down in the rhythm of her words, and it didn't matter what she was saying, the voice wafted down and covered me like arms. A couple walked by holding hands and smiled at us and I thought, *my God, that couple is us. We are them*. For once, for the first time in my life, I felt loved.

I didn't see Vespucci coming. There was no portent of evil rushing my way, no accumulation of dark clouds on my horizon. As I said, things were good. I had been loading beer for several months, piling the cases onto pallets, spreading shrink-wrap around the cases, and hauling the pallets onto the trucks. It was difficult but fulfilling work, the kind that exhausts and exhilarates at the same time. I was good at it, my arms having grown strong in Cox's living room and the weight room at Waxham.

The way it worked was one shipping boy was assigned to one truck driver on each load, working until the truck was filled and ready to depart. Then the next truck would come in, get loaded, and take off. There was no order to the trucks, and we would work with nearly all the drivers in the course of a week. The aspiration of the shipping boys was eventually to get to drive the trucks, which meant greater pay and at least part of your day in the air-conditioning or out of the rain. When a driving vacancy occurred, Father Steve's brother promoted from within based on driver recommendations. This meant all the shipping boys busted their asses for all the drivers, so coveted were those recommendations. It was a good system.

One of the drivers was Hap Blowenfeld, and every shipping boy looked up to Hap the way some people look up to movie stars and ball players. He was larger-than-life, with perfect hair, a quick smile, and pearl white teeth. He had huge arms, could load a truck faster than anyone, and bought a six-pack of Coke for the shipping boy who helped him each day. The day you got assigned to Hap was like winning the lottery, and if you got him twice in one week, you were the envy of every other shipper in the crew.

'What's your story, Buck?' he asked me after I had worked there a couple of months. We were loading Budweiser, and it was hot outside. We hadn't said much to each other, both concentrating on stacking the cases on to the wooden pallets. I wasn't much of a talker, and the question caught me off guard.

'No story,' was all I could mumble.

Hap looked up with the hint of a grin, his arm leaning on one of the beer cases. 'I'll let you in on a little secret. I spent my time in Juvenile too.'

I didn't say anything.

'That's right,' he said, starting to lift the cases again. 'Five years in a place called Skyline Hall in Sacramento for choking a kid to death. I grew up on the West Coast, in Arcadia, outside Los Angeles, went to school with mostly Mexicans. Well, this one bean-eater stole my daddy's billfold, and I didn't like that too much. I didn't know I'd kill't the poor bastard until someone pried my fingers off his throat.' He stopped and wiped his head with the back of his hand. 'I was thirteen years old. I thought I was gonna play college football.'

I didn't know what to say, and for a moment we resumed loading the crates onto the pallets and the pallets onto the truck in our comfortable rhythm. I was beginning to think maybe Hap's story was all in my head. He broke the silence again.

'So what's your story, Crackerjack? And don't go soft on me.'

Hap wasn't the kind of guy I was prepared to lie to, so I just spread it out before him like I was unfolding a map, starting with my first venture inside the Cox house and finishing with my release from Waxham. Before I knew it, my story was over, the truck was completely loaded, and Hap and I were leaning against the back bumper sipping Coke out of bottles through pharmacy straws.

'You didn't kill him?' Hap asked, gnawing on his lower lip a little bit.

I shook my head side to side.

'But you wanted to.'

'Yep.'

'I'd've liked to get my hands on that sum-bitch.' He stared down at his hands, as though he could see it happening, what Cox's throat would look like caught in his massive fingers, squeezing the neck until it caved in on itself.

Hap looked at me sideways. 'You think you had it in you to finish him?'

'If I could've, I would've.'

Hap grinned. 'I'll bet you would. I just bet you would.'

He drove off a few minutes later, and I went to get my next assignment, feeling a slight pull in my chest.

A week later, I had completely forgotten about my conversation with Hap when a Cadillac limousine pulled alongside me while I was walking home from work. A dark window slid down and an olive, moon-shaped face stared out at me. I thought this man must have mistaken me for someone, the way Jake had mistaken me for her brother. A fat hand extended out the window toward me.

'Vespucci,' the face said, the hand waiting in anticipation.

I shook it, unsure what to say.

Then a second face filled the window behind Vespucci's, with a broad grin and a wink aimed in my direction. 'Get in, Buck,' Hap said, as the door opened my way.

The car was bigger than anything I had seen before, like the inside of the empty beer trucks, and I sat facing the dark Italian and Hap. Their eyes studied my face like they were trying to read a book; what exactly they were hoping to find in my expression, I had no idea. Waxham had taught me to suppress my emotions, to make my face as blank as fresh paper, and for a long moment we rode in silence, measuring each other.

'You some kind of orphan?' the dark face asked in a thick Italian accent.

'Yes.'

'Yes, what, kid?' Hap corrected, his face urging me.

'Yes, sir,' I said, not wanting to disappoint Hap.

'Good. Dat's good, kid. What's your name?'

I answered him and he laughed. 'You get a new name starting today. A new name when you work for me.'

I had no idea what this man was talking about.

'Work for you?'

'Dat's right. Starting today.'

I looked at Hap, and he just nodded at me, smiling, like he had done me a great favour.

The car pulled up alongside an abandoned warehouse, a large building in a part of town I had never visited. The building took up a city block, and was probably once teeming with factory workers and sweat and life, but now just stood blank and forgotten, like an old man put to rest in a nursing home. The windows in the upper stories looked shattered, and natty birds flew in and out intermittently. On the side of the building, 'Columbus Textiles' was printed in faded block letters.

'But first, a test,' Vespucci said. 'To see what kind of . . . possibility . . . you might have.' He seemed to linger over the word 'possibility' like it tasted sweet in his mouth and he was savouring it. 'Let's go.'

Inside the warehouse, dust settled over what little furniture had been left behind when the company packed up and moved. The place had once been used to make textiles, and inoperative looms and abandoned sewing machines lay dormant on the tops of forgotten tabletops. The main room was huge, like a cathedral, and a small desk had been recently pushed to the middle of the floor. On top of the desk lay a pistol.

'What is this?' I asked, puzzled, searching for answers in the faces of the men who'd brought me here. If those faces held answers, I wasn't experienced enough to read them.

Just then, another door opened on the other side of the enormous room. Three men approached us, their hollow footsteps clomping over the concrete floor, but in the dim light of the room I couldn't make out their features. One of the men, though, had a hauntingly familiar gait, a way of walking as unique and identifiable as a fingerprint.

'What is this, Hap?'

Then a voice I had tried to forget so many times reached out and punched me in the gut like a fist. 'Yeah,' said Pete Cox, representing the middle of the trio who approached. 'What the fuck is this? These two fellas promised me there was something I'd . . . want . . . to . . . see . . .'

His eyes found mine, and for a moment he was as surprised as I was. He said my name, then repeated it, dumbfounded, like he was waking from a dream. Then he looked over his shoulder at the two men flanking him, their eyes as hard as concrete. 'What is this?' he repeated, weakly.

'This,' said Vespucci in a rough growl, 'is a test.'

'A what?' said Cox, like he didn't hear the man correctly.

'A test for the boy you liked knocking around so much, tough guy.'

Cox's eyes settled on the pistol resting on the desk and he started backpedalling, his feet moving almost involuntarily. But the two men closed on him, and held him firmly by the elbows so he could no longer move.

'Hey, wait, what's this . . . ? What's this all about? He . . . he killed my wife. Did he tell you that?' His voice sounded shrill.

Hap spat on the ground. 'He told me everything I needed to know.'

I still couldn't find my voice . . . this clash with my past jarring me as though I'd been shell-shocked. Here was Mr Cox, the man who had caused an enormous abyss in my childhood, standing before me. The only item positioned between us was a pistol.

Vespucci spoke. 'In ten seconds, my men and I are going to leave this place and lock the door behind us. On that desk is a pistol. Somewhere in this room are the bullets that can be fired from that pistol. I will open the doors again tomorrow morning and only one of you will come out. If there are two of you standing here when I open the door, I'll cut you both down. Only one walks out tomorrow morning.'

I looked at Mr Cox's face with what must have been a feral snarl and I could almost feel him reeling back, looking for an escape route.

'You must be joking. I can't . . .' he started to protest, but every man in the room besides us turned on their heels and headed for the exits, leaving the sentence to die in the air, unfinished. We both stood silently, as two sets of doors swung shut and were bolted behind us. Neither of us flinched, nor twitched a muscle; we just stared at each other.

Then as the weight of the silence threatened to crush us, he leaped for the gun. My legs took over, and I tackled him before his hand could grip the weapon. We smashed into the desk, overturning it, and the gun skittered across the floor.

His hands went for my face, trying to claw my eyes as we both fought for leverage. He was still bigger than me, and his legs straddled mine, so I couldn't gain my balance, while his hands continued to scratch at my face. The only thing I could do was ball my hands into fists and start driving my knuckles into his rib cage, his kidneys, one, two, three times, again and again. He may have had a weight advantage, but I had learned a great deal about dirty fighting in the exercise

57

yard at Waxham. I must have caught him under a rib, because suddenly he gasped for breath and fell over sideways.

I sprang up, my eyes a bit blurry from the pressure, and stumbled toward the gun. He caught his breath and stood to follow, just as I scooped up the weapon.

As I held it up, he sneered, 'Lot of good that will do you without the—' But before he could finish that thought, I pistol-whipped him across the face, smashing him so hard his mouth filled with blood and he fell to the floor in a heap. He started to rise, so I smashed him again harder, putting all my weight behind it, and this time he stayed down. Faint whimpers came from his throat and quickly died in the large, hollow room.

Fuck the bullets. I headed for an old rusty sewing machine that looked like it hadn't been used in decades. It must have weighed over fifty pounds, but it seemed light as a feather as I hoisted it onto my shoulder and marched back toward the whimpering heap on the floor.

He looked up as I stood over him, gore splashed all over his lips, his gums, his teeth. 'Wha-what are you doing this for?' he sobbed.

'For Pooley,' I said, and smashed the sewing machine down on top of his skull.

I sit in my hotel room in Philadelphia watching Abe Mann outline his vision for America on television. This is how he will sit, I imagine, a few weeks from now, watching himself say the same things by rote, over and over. How he's for working families, and lower taxes, and cutting tax breaks for the rich. How he's for a woman's right to choose and a stronger military and jobs staying home instead of going overseas. The same fast-food dish served up stale by politicians every few years.

His voice is throaty; it arrives from deep down in his lungs. It is one of the reasons he has been so successful in politics: he is well-practised in *how* he speaks, even if he doesn't believe *what* he is saying. And he has a new handgesture: an open palm, the fingers splayed, shaking at an angle as he punctuates the key words in his speech. It is a variation on the thumb-point, or the crooked index finger. It gives him a certain authority, like an old Southern preacher at the pulpit. I find myself making the same gesture with my hand, watching him without listening, the way he does while he speaks.

The phone rings, and it is Pooley on the other end when I answer.

'What did you find?'

'Very little, so far. Archibald Grant has disappeared; no one has seen him in days.'

'Then whoever hired me has tossed his middleman.'

'Looks that way.'

My mind is racing. 'What next, then?'

Pooley blew out a long breath. 'I'm going to dig some more, see if I can't find a trail from Grant to someone else.'

'You sure you want to do that?'

'Hey . . . why should you be the only one who gets to climb out from behind a desk?'

I smile. 'You be careful.'

'You got it.'


I am on the road again, back in my element, the present. I am heading to Ohio, what they call a battleground state, where Abe Mann will spend an unprecedented three days on his tour . . . Cleveland, then Dayton, then Cincinnati. Electoral votes in this state have swung an election in the past, and glad-handing is necessary and expected. I try to imagine what Abe Mann will be feeling at this point in the campaign. Fatigue? Irritation? Or will he feel re-newed, as I do now? Back in the present. Yesterday behind me.

In Cleveland, I eat lunch at a restaurant called Augustine's. It is upscale but strives to be better than it is, like a scarred woman who puts on too much rouge to cover her blemishes. The food is bland and tasteless. A young couple at a table next to me is talking about the upcoming election, and without turning my head I can hear every word they say. Or rather I can hear every word *she* says, since she is dominating the conversation.

'I consider myself socially liberal but economically conservative. Winston Churchill once said, "If you're young and a conservative, you have no heart. But if

you're old and a democrat, you have no money."'
The man across from her chuckles. 'But I'm being serious here. I feel like we pay way too much in taxes, and for what? More Washington waste?'

'So you're voting Republican?' the man asks.

'No, I'm still undecided. I want to hear what the candidates have to say at their conventions and then . . .'

Her voice continues on and on, like a comfortable hum, and it strikes me that this woman is the same age Jake would be. Now, I know I shouldn't turn my head, I know I definitely should *not* make eye contact, but there is something in her voice that washes over me like warm water. I stick out my index finger and clumsily knock my fork off the table, toward the woman's voice. We both reach for it at the same time, and for a full second, we look into each other's faces. I don't know what she finds in mine, but in hers I see what might have been.

# Chapter Five

My first paying job for Vespucci was to kill a woman.
He was waiting in my apartment on a Sunday after-
noon, after I had spent the day walking around the
Harbor with Jake. His face was grave, serious.

'Do you know what a fence is, Columbus?' He had
been calling me 'Columbus' since the door swung
open at the abandoned Columbus Textile warehouse
the morning after I had brained Mr Cox.

'No, sir. Not any other way than what I think it is.'

'I am a fence. A fence is a middleman. A go-
between. Do you understand?'

I looked at him with what I am sure was a blank
expression.

'I am hired by certain people for the purpose of
assassination. They give me a target's name. It is my
job as the fence to find out as much information about
the mark as I can. Then I, in turn, assign the job to

one of my professionals. The professional never meets the client. That is my job. Do you understand?'

'I think so.'

'Good, Columbus. You are . . . a quick learner.'

'And I'm your professional?'

He chortled a little. 'Not yet, no. You are . . . how should I say . . . an understudy, like in the theatre. You will learn your role and be ready to fill a position as necessary. You will be paid only if you kill a mark. And once you're paid,' he said, a broad smile appearing across his face, 'well, then, I suppose you are a professional.'

I moved to the kitchen and took down a box of crackers from a shelf. But I only fidgeted with the box, turning it over and over in my hands like a pig on a spit.

'What if I'm not interested in being one of your professionals?'

He cleared his throat, covering his mouth with his fist, and the smile left his face. 'God gave you free will. I do not presume to take that away from you. However, I have looked into your eyes, Columbus. I have seen the orphan childhood; I have felt your hands turn into fists. You are a killer. A . . . how is it . . . a natural killer. The warehouse didn't make you a killer. You were one before you ever lifted that sewing machine above your head. I only helped show you what you are.'

I set the box of crackers down on the counter in front of me. There was a ringing in my ears, and I'm not sure if it was fear, or the fact I had heard the sound of truth delivered by this dark Italian in my kitchen.

'Hap saw something in you . . . saw this quality. He saw it . . . instinctively. He thought you could do this job after one conversation with you.'

'He works for you, then?'

'I have many people who work for me.' He studied me for a moment, appraising me. 'I have a feeling. I have a feeling I would have found you anyway. There is a level to . . . how do you say . . . to fate? Yes? It causes paths to cross in ways we cannot understand.' He stopped, waving his hand, like he had stumbled down a dark road and now wanted to reverse direction. He handed me a manila envelope, the kind you might find in any office storage closet. A ten-by-thirteen plain manila envelope, heavy and rigid. 'Read this,' he said, 'then we'll talk. Tomorrow, perhaps.'

With that, he put on his hat and shuffled toward the door.

I spent hours poring over the contents of that envelope, exhilarated, like a person entrusted with a singular and dangerous confidence. The first sheet held a name printed in big black letters across the top: Michael Folio. There was an address: 1022 South Holt Ave., and a description: six-two, 200 pounds, medium build, sandy hair, wire-frame glasses, no tattoos, no birthmarks. And there was more: 'Michael has a facial tic that causes his upper lip to curl at the right corner. He has no relatives except a sister who lives in British Columbia, Carol Dougherty. She is married to Frank Dougherty, a plumber, and has two kids, Shawn, ten, and Carla, eight. They have not corresponded with Michael in over seven years.'

The next page gave a detailed description of Michael's office: 'He is a litigator in the law firm Douglas and Thackery. His office is on the fifth floor of a five-story office complex known as The Meadows. The firm has 25 employees. They are: Carol Santree, receptionist . . .' This type of thing. The third page provided a blueprint of the office with a seating chart as to where exactly each employee sat. The fourth page gave a chronological list of precisely where Michael had been over the last thirty days: '8 A.M., target leaves house, moving West on Holt. He stops at Starbucks on corner of Holt and Landover. 8:15 A.M., leaves Starbucks continues west on Holt, follows until he reaches Highway 765, then turns north.'

This description continued for the next thirty pages or so. It began to dawn on me the time and energy and man-hours it took to compile the pages I held in my hands. Why would I need to know that working in his office was a junior partner named Sam Goodwin? That Michael frequently ate his lunch alone at The Olive Garden? That the route he took to get to the cleaners involved a shortcut on Romero Street? But the answer was obvious . . . so I, as the assassin assigned the task of killing Michael Folio, would best

66

be able to plan my attack and my escape. Since I know that when he finishes his meal at The Olive Garden, eighty-seven percent of the time he uses the bathroom on his way out the door, I could plan to wait and ambush him in the men's room stall. Since I know that he hasn't spoken to his niece and nephew in seven years, I could pretend to be a friend of theirs and 'bump' into him next to the dry cleaners. Gain his trust and get invited into his home. The possibilities were endless, but only because I had this file Vespucci had meticulously laboured over.

That's when the addiction began. I studied those pages as though I was reading scripture, each line read and read and read again until Michael Folio's life was committed to memory. I found myself thinking of little else, waiting for the phone to ring.

We were eating lunch when I saw him. Jake had ordered breadsticks and salad and was picking away through her meal, while I was waiting on the pasta I had ordered.

'I'd like you to come home with me for the holidays,' she said, looking at me through the tops of her eyes.

'I thought you weren't interested in seeing your family.'

'I didn't think I was. And I don't know why, but they *are* my family and for some inexplicable reason I feel compelled to see them over the holidays. Maybe there's something to be said for nature and nurture and all that sociological bullshit we studied my freshman year. If you don't want to go, you don't have to . . . I'd understand.'

'Why wouldn't I want to go?'

She smiled. 'I don't know. I just assumed you wouldn't want to . . .'

'You still don't have me figured out, do you?' I said.

'Every time I think I do, you throw me a curveball.'

She settled into her food again, and I looked at the door, and that's when I saw him. Michael Folio. The man from the envelope. The man who was going to die as soon as Vespucci gave the word. He waited at the hostess stand, then held up one finger, and the hostess nodded and led him toward a booth halfway between the bathroom and the table where Jake and I sat. I had purposely picked a table so I could sit with my back to the wall. That way, I would have a view of the entire restaurant.

Jake started talking again, but I didn't hear what she was saying because a buzzing nested in my ear as I watched Michael Folio – not just a picture on top of a sheet of paper but a living and breathing human being. He sat down and studied his menu.

Jake turned her head to see what had gotten my attention. She probably thought I was staring at a woman, but when she saw a man in a suit and tie, she said, 'You know him?'

I shook my head. 'What?'

'That man . . . you looked at him like you knew him.'

'Did I?' I laughed. 'I blanked out wondering where the hell my food was.'

That did the trick. She went back to talking about her family, and my food arrived, and I twirled the noodles around my fork and tried to concentrate, but every few seconds my eyes drifted to the breathing dead-man seated alone in the middle of the restaurant.

Finally, I excused myself and walked toward the bathroom. I had to pass by his booth on the way, and I glanced down at him as I went, but he didn't notice. He was reading a copy of *Sports Illustrated*, engrossed in an article.

Inside the bathroom, I stared at myself in the mirror, trying to get my body to stop shaking. This was a new sensation; I felt electric, like a brewing storm. I splashed some water on my face, was rubbing my eyes, when the door to the bathroom opened.

I half-expected to see Michael Folio come through the door; in fact, I had planned my trip to the bathroom to coincide with the waitress bringing him his bill. But instead of Folio, it was Vespucci's large figure who shuffled through the door. His eyes glowered at me, like they wanted to pick me up and throw me across the room.

'What're you doing?' he spat in a hushed tone.

'Nothing. I—'

'You were to do *nothing* until I gave you the command. What you are doing here is not nothing!'

'I'm doing my homework, in case you called.'

'Homework? Don't bullshit me.'

'That's all I was doing.'

'Who's the girl?'

'What? She's just a girl I know.'

'You like her?'

'She's just a girl, Mr Vespucci.'

'We'll talk about this later. Pay your bill and go home.'

I knew this was not open for discussion. I nodded, shimmied past him, and headed back to the restaurant. As I passed Folio's booth, I noticed he was gone. Jake looked at me concerned as I approached our table.

'What's wrong?'

'I'm not feeling well.'

'Oh, I'm sorry. Do you think it was the pasta?'

'I don't know. We just need to go.'

She stood up, sympathy on her face. 'You just head to the car. I'll get the check.'

She drove me home while I pretended to feel queasy. It wasn't difficult, since I was thinking about how upset Vespucci had been, how his eyes had flashed when he entered the bathroom. She dropped me off and I protested against her coming in with me . . . saying I needed to be alone and get this worked out. Reluctantly, she let me go, and I noticed it was several minutes before her car moved away from the curb.

Vespucci didn't come that night, or the next day, or the second night. I talked to Jake a couple of times and told her it was nothing but a stomach flu, that I would be fine, that I just felt weak and begged off meeting up with her for a few days. She wanted to take care of me, and I think she was saddened that I refused her succour. I think this might have raised the first questions in her mind as to where our relationship was going.

I more or less had the radio on all day, just background noise to keep me company as I waited. Which is why at first I didn't process the report about the litigator who had been shot while sitting at his desk on the fifth floor of the Meadows Office Complex in the northern part of the city. The reporter's words were just a dull hum when the name 'Michael Folio' broke through the clutter. I leapt up like I was on fire and raced to the radio, turning the volume up as loud as it would go. The reporter was talking about another D.C. sniper, right here in Boston. Police were speculating that the bullet must have come from a neighbouring rooftop and had caught the litigator just above his right ear as he sat reading a briefing at his desk. His assistant had heard the sound of glass shatter-

71

ing and had rushed to his office, only to find him lying facedown on his desk in a pool of his own blood. There was no more news at this time.

Just then, my door opened and Vespucci showed himself inside. He nodded at the radio, 'You heard?'

I nodded back.

'Who was the girl?'

'A girl I've been seeing.'

'Get rid of her.'

'Why?'

'Don't ask me why. You know why without me telling you.'

He dropped a new envelope on my counter and sat down on top of a bar stool.

'Mr Vespucci . . . what I do on my own time is my business . . . now I don't mind—'

He cut me off. 'You think you are the first one to do this job? To be a professional?'

'I don't—'

'There are reasons why I picked you. Number one. No father and mother. Number two. No father and mother. Do I make sense? Yes?'

I stood there, smarting.

'Relationships are weakness. In this line of work, you can have no weakness. Or, I assure you, your weakness will be discovered and exploited.'

'By whom?'

'By whom?' he snorted. 'I forget what a babe you

are. You are now in the business of killing men. Women and children too, if that is your assignment. When you do this job, you make enemies. Enemies in law enforcement, enemies in the families of the person you kill, enemies who are rival assassins. Yes. That's right. I am not the only fence in this country; not even in this city. There are others who will do whatever they can to stop you from continuing to do what you do. And they will find this girl and exploit her. I promise you that.'

'She's the first girl—'

'What? Who cared for you? Who made love to you? Bah. Let me tell you this, Columbus . . . she is nothing but a weight on your chest, pushing down on your breastbone, crushing the wind out of you. You *must* let her go. Tell her you will never see her again. I can give you no better advice than this.'

'I understand.'

'We're in agreement, then?'

'I said I understand.'

I said it passionately too, and he stared at me for a long time, measuring me, trying to read my thoughts. I diverted my eyes and picked up the envelope.

'What's this, then?'

'Your next mark.'

'Will I get a chance to prove myself this time?'

Vespucci stood up. 'That is not up to me.'

'Who is it up to, then?'

'To God, I suppose. Study the contents of that

73

envelope.' He made it to the door. 'And forget this girl, Columbus.'

He didn't wait for my reply as he shuffled out into the hall.

The name at the top of the page in the second envelope was Edgar Schmidt, a police detective. I did not get the call to kill him, but read about his death on the front page of the *Globe* three weeks later. The third envelope contained the name Wilson Montgomery, a pipefitter who had dealings with the mob. He died a week later, though I never found out how. The fourth envelope was devoted to a man named Seamus O'Dooley, a nightclub owner. He was gunned down in the alley behind his establishment.

I studied all of these files with undiminished intensity. In fact, each time I wasn't called in to complete the mission only served to make me more focused on the next file.

But I didn't forget the girl, despite what Vespucci ordered of me. I wanted to please him, but I wasn't about to cast off the only part of my life that had ever meant anything. So when the holidays rolled around, Jake and I took off in her little Honda for New Hampshire.

Her family met us at the door. Her father, Jim, took my hand and warmly pumped it as he guided us into the house. In the fireplace, warm flames licked the screen that kept the embers at bay. The house was rustic, like many of the homes dotting the New England countryside, and the inside was filled with wooden Western-style furniture. A brown leather sofa took up most of the living room, and the home felt as warm as the fire. It was a home, a real *home*, something I'd never experienced.

Her mother, Molly, studied my face, a broad smile on her own, and said, 'Well, don't just stand there, Jim, grab his bag. We're gonna put you in Louis's room. It gets a little cold at night, but we'll throw some extra blankets on your bed and you'll be snug as a bug.' It seemed that once Jake's mother opened her mouth, she couldn't stop the onslaught of words tumbling from it.

Jake smiled and rolled her eyes when Molly wasn't looking, as if to say 'I tried to warn you . . .'

The food covering the dining table was enough to feed a dozen people: peaches wrapped with prosciutto, a warm pear-and-endive salad, a honey-baked ham with a brown-sugar crust, baked beans, and no less than three pies waiting on a side table: pumpkin, key lime, and buttermilk chess.

'Jake tells us you work for a distribution company?' Jim asked when we had stacked our plates.

'Yes, sir. It's just a start until I can earn enough money to begin school.'

'Oh?' Molly said, more of a comment than a question.

'Yes, ma'am. I didn't—'

Jake rescued me. 'Mother—'

'What? I didn't say anything.'

I looked at Jake and nodded, like I had this under control. 'My parents died when I was an infant, and I was raised in foster homes, though not by parents you would call "loving". So if I want to go to college, it's up to me to pay for it. And I don't believe in owing the government a nickel, so, like I said, I'm just building up my account.'

Jim cast a stern eye at his wife, then looked back at me. 'Well, I think that is not only a refreshing attitude but an admirable one.' He deftly changed the subject . . . 'Well, what did you think of the drive into Nashua? Jake always likes to come in the back way, but I've been saying for years the Interstate can slice twenty minutes off . . .'

'Jesus, Daddy, you're embarrassing me!' she squealed happily and tossed her napkin at him.

The conversation stayed in the mundane, and Molly didn't let anything dampen her ability to dominate a conversation. Her sentences ran together without punctuation . . . I'm not even sure she took breaths. But I loved every minute of it . . . the food, the conversation, the family, and Jake's hand that made its way under the table to mine. She squeezed it in three pulses, as if to say 'I love you', and I believed she did, believed it like I had never believed anything. And I started to think, we could be like this, Jake and me, thirty years from now, talking over a table to our own child and her new boyfriend. We could be having a meal like this.

I left the light on next to my bed so I could read the latest file Vespucci handed me before I left. He had been in the hallway when I returned from a hard run, and I didn't invite him in. I don't know why I didn't, or even if he gave a shit. He just waited for a second, studied my face, and when I didn't extend the invitation, he turned and left. I had the feeling he knew I was still seeing Jake, that I was going to be out of town that weekend, but I didn't open my mouth to confirm it. Hell, if he wanted me to kill for him, I wasn't giving this up. And if we never talked about it again, that was all right by me.

The name at the top of the file was Janet Stephens. She was a judge in the 5th Circuit Court, City of Boston. She was not married, but had an ongoing relationship with a female attorney named Mary Gibbons. She lived in a town house in the Back Bay, not far from Beacon Street, with a corgi named Dusty. The courthouse was downtown, a twenty-minute walk through the Common from her front gate.

The picture of Janet revealed a middle-aged woman with a broad forehead and cocoa skin. Her father was black and her mother was white, and she had that beautiful tone found in a lot of offspring of mixed parentage. Her eyes were a piercing shade of green, and her hair fell in tight dark curls down to her chin. Her nose was disproportionately big, however, and it marred what was otherwise a handsome face. She stayed in shape too, working out five days a week with a personal trainer . . . alternating upper and lower body workouts with cardio training each session. Her gym was equidistant between her town home and her courtroom.

Now, whether there was a hit on her because she sent the wrong guy up or because she was about to preside over an important trial, I didn't have the slightest idea. Maybe the contract on her life had nothing to do with her job. Again, I didn't know. My middleman made sure I stayed in the dark. It kept curiosity at bay, like a leash on an angry dog. The less we knew about the 'why's', the less tempted we were to learn more about our clients. It was just an assignment, an impersonal killing, something I was expected to do by rote.

I was sleeping a dreamless sleep when Jim's voice cut through the darkness. He said something about the phone, and it took me a moment to realize he was standing in the doorway with a cordless receiver in his hand.

'I'm sorry . . . ?' I asked, still trying to shake out the cobwebs.

'There's a gentleman on the phone for you. He said it was urgent.'

Waking in this bed, in this room, at this time was so foreign, it didn't register to me what was happening as I sat up in the bed and Jim handed me the receiver. He backed out of the room to give me some privacy.

'Hello?' I said into the phone, my eyes still adjusting to the darkness.

Vespucci's voice reached through the receiver. 'It's a go.'

*Vespucci. He had found me. He knew exactly what I was up to, had even obtained the home number to Jake's parents' house. The middleman, the fence, whose job it was to find out everything he could about a target, had also found out everything he could about me.* These thoughts were ripping through my head in an instant, only to be broken when the dark Italian spoke again. 'Twenty-four hours.' And then the phone clicked off.

*It's a go. Twenty-four hours.* Six words packed with a meaning that stretched all the way from this bedroom to a town house off of Beacon Street. I stood up, suddenly awake, as though smelling salts had been twirled under my nose, and started to dress.

When I came out of the bedroom, carrying my pack, Jim was stooped over a pot of coffee, pouring it into two large mugs.

'I'm sorry the call woke you,' I offered.

He handed me a mug. 'I'm a hopeless insomniac,' he said, taking a sip of his coffee. 'I usually get up by four. It gives me time to think.'

'What time is it now?' The coffee tasted very good.

'Four,' he said, a twinkle to his eye. 'You need to split?'

'Yes, sir. Something came up at work. They need me to fill in.'

'No problem. Take the mug with you.'

'I couldn't—'

'Don't be silly.'

Just then, Jake's voice cut through the quiet of the room. 'What's going on?' she managed. She looked beautiful, standing in an over-sized nightshirt, rubbing the sleep out of her eyes. Looking at her there, it was all I could do to speak.

'I'm sorry . . . I got an emergency call. Everyone's calling in sick to work today and they need me to fill in. Must be the flu or something. But they said it would be double pay if I could get there by seven. I can't pass it up.'

She yawned and looked at her dad. 'Any more of that java?'

'Half a pot.'

'Well then, pour me a mug while I get dressed, old man.'

'You don't have to go. I'll just call a cab to take me to a rental car place. Company said they'd pay for it.'

She moved over and kissed me on the lips, sleepily, right in front of her dad. 'Don't be silly,' she said, sounding just like her father. 'I'll drive you. Pop . . . apologize to Mom for us.'

★   ★   ★

We rode most of the way talking about innocuous things . . . my impression of her parents, the neighbourhood, the house, the bed, the dinner. I was glad not to have to concentrate on what we were saying; my thoughts were on the file in my backpack.

When we arrived at my front stoop, I kissed her on the cheek, mumbled a few words of thanks, and hurried up into my apartment without looking back. Already, my heart was beating as though it had been shocked with a charger. I made my way to my closet and selected a pair of brown slacks and a long-sleeved white shirt. Over this, I pulled down a navy blue blazer. The same clothes fifty thousand men in Boston were putting on at that very moment. Nothing memorable, nothing that stood out. There is a way of dressing, of walking, of casting your eyes, that people looking right at you don't even register your presence. This is a skill boys learn at Waxham, another reason I'm sure Hap recommended me to Vespucci.

I eased open the suitcase I kept under the bed. Inside, the tools of my trade, given to me by Vespucci when I stepped out of the Columbus Textile warehouse: a Glock 17 semi automatic pistol; a box of fifty 9-millimetre hollow point bullets; a serrated knife with a spiked handle; a cache of false ID's, credit cards, business cards. In case I was struck down doing my duty, my identity would be difficult to determine, giving Vespucci enough time to cover his tracks, probably by burning down this apartment.

I had not graduated yet to a sniper rifle, and though I am semi-proficient in its use now, it is not my preferred *modus operandi*. There is an adage that says the closer you can get to a mark, the more skilled you are as an assassin, but I think that adage is as porous as a sieve. Some of the dumbest killers in the world have stood two feet from their prey and pulled the trigger, and some of the most skilled riflemen have toppled their marks from distances greater than five city blocks. A close-contact killer may have to negotiate startled bystanders, while a marksman has to balance wind speed, sunlight, elements, obstructions, and the occasional spotter. Each takes expert skill. The trick, even as green as I was then, was to get in a position that would give me the most comfort . . . comfort in locating the target, comfort in killing the target, and comfort in escaping from the murder scene directly after the assassination.

I was standing near a bus stop on Beacon Street, reading the *Globe* like any other bored commuter, checking my watch occasionally, humming to myself a bland tune. The door to Janet Stephens's town house opened and she emerged, wearing a navy dress and white walking sneakers for her short hike to the courthouse.

As soon as she entered the Common, I folded my paper, tucked it under my arm, and followed from thirty yards away, adjusting my pace to match hers, so that we would remain the same distance apart. I felt certain that somewhere Vespucci was watching me like the eye of God to see how his newest charge would handle the pressure of his first assignment.

Janet passed a couple of tourists looking at the duck sculptures, then took a left down one of the paths dissecting the park. She walked at a pace somewhere between brisk and leisurely, not enough to break a sweat but quick enough to keep me on my toes. I could feel my pulse rising in my ears, like a phantom drumbeat, pounding, pounding. The middle of her back stayed tight as she swung her arms, and it seemed wider than the way it was described in the file, certainly wide enough to hit, to split open, to shatter the spine, even from thirty yards away.

She slowed as she left the park and came to a crosswalk. A blinking red hand on the light-box across the street forced her to a stop, and she used the chance to stoop down and tie a loose shoelace. I had no choice but to approach the same crosswalk; there were several other pedestrians also waiting for the light to change, so it wasn't as though I would be the only one joining her on the corner.

Still, it seemed like a giant spotlight was trained right on me. I looked past the businessman in front of me and concentrated on the middle of Janet Stephens's back, less than two feet away now, stooped over, the cloth on her dress fluttering slightly as she tightened the lace. Two feet away. The Glock felt heavy where it hugged my ribs, hidden behind the loose-fitting blazer. I scratched my belly with my right hand, a casual gesture, then reached further in my jacket, as though I were scratching a rib. The metal of the gun barrel felt cold on my fingertips. Right now. I could do it right here, at the corner of the park, pull the gun, and then . . .

The blinking red hand changed to the universal sign for 'walk'. Janet sprung up and quickly returned to her previous pace. I let the other commuters pass in front of me and held back until I had returned to a comfortable distance. I was still thirty yards behind when Janet Stephens disappeared up the steps of the courthouse.

Was Vespucci watching? Did he see me hesitate and make a mental note, maybe even write something down in a notebook? Was he judging me, right now, this instant? 'Columbus hesitated. A waste of an opportunity. Will need to cut him down first chance.'

Pushing these thoughts aside, I made my way down the street and stepped into a Korean grocery . . . a place as dark and dirty as a gopher's hole. The shelves had a caked-on layer of dust that hadn't felt the underside of a wet cloth in months. I picked up a box of Saran Wrap and then dropped the box on to the ground, like it had slipped from my fingers. As quick as lightning, I snatched the gun from its holster and slipped it into the crack between the lowest shelf and the floor. Same with the serrated knife. They might need a strong cleaning when I retrieved them later, but I wasn't worried that the Korean woman in the back was going to find them while sweeping. I don't think this floor had seen a broom in ages. With the knife and gun tucked out of sight, I picked up the box like nothing had happened, took it to the front, paid for it so as not to raise suspicion, and headed back into the sunlight.

The entrance to the courthouse funnelled into a metal detector, marked by three security guards and a red rope cordon. I put my recently purchased Saran Wrap and keys into a tray and then walked through the detector, eyes cast low. I didn't look the security guard in the eye as he handed back my belongings, just took them perfunctorily and headed toward a cluster of elevators where a small crowd had congregated. From my file, I knew Judge Janet Stephens's courtroom was on the sixth floor. I also knew Judge Janet Stephens never took the elevator; she always climbed the stairs, part of her exercise regimen.

Just then, a curt voice from near the elevators shook the lobby: 'Jury duty, report to the sixth floor. End of the hall on the right. Jury duty, sixth floor, end of the hall on the right.'

I scanned the crowd, a varied group of vapid stares, people who looked like they'd rather be anywhere else. The kind of crowd you could sit with all day and no one would remember you.

The jury room was huge, and there were easily five hundred people inside. We were supposed to fill out cards and hand them in to the female administrator up near the front of the room, and then she would draw names for each pool. I took a seat in the back of the room without filling out a card. The only thing that concerned me was remaining anonymous and keeping an eye on the clock. Eleven-thirty. I knew from the file that on most days, Janet Stephens called recess at eleven-thirty.

The courtroom emptied at three minutes past the hour. I had been loitering for thirty minutes, trying not to look out of place, but it wasn't difficult to blend into the surroundings. There were three courtrooms on the sixth floor and people scurried to and from each like rodents trying to stay out of the light. Nobody wanted to be seen and nobody wanted to make eye contact with anyone else. The hall remained as quiet as a museum; the only sounds were the occasional clicking of a woman's heels, some defendant's wife or girlfriend trying to look her best for her man and the jury. Everyone spoke in whispers, like somehow, if they showed deference to this place, they might find themselves treated fairly.

The occupants of the courtroom – the jurors, attorneys, stenographers, bailiffs – all made their way to the elevator bank soon after the doors to the courtroom thrust open, heading out for their designated one-hour lunch. I moved over to the stairwell and disappeared inside.

Quickly, I moved to the fifth-floor landing and waited. I would need a little luck, just a little.

After a few minutes, I heard the stairwell door open above me. From Janet Stephens's file, I knew she liked to eat each day at the deli down on the northwest corner of the courthouse building. She always ordered steamed vegetables and brown rice, and ate quietly as she read over her morning paperwork. I also knew she never failed to avoid the elevators in favour of the stairs. It is routines like this – the mundane, the boring, the normal, people caught in a rut – that make it easy for an assassin to do his job.

I heard the door creak closed followed by the soft shuffle of white tennis shoes on the concrete stairs. My heart was pounding in my ears, loud percussive blasts like an Indian's tom-tom, TUM, TUM, TUM, TUM, TUM, as I blew out a deep breath, doing my best to regulate my breathing, then I headed up toward the sixth floor.

We both turned the corner on the short flight of twelve steps between the fifth and sixth floor. She directed a dismissive smile toward me, averting her eyes like she really didn't want to talk to a juror or some poor lost bloke in the stairwell while she was on her way to lunch. I didn't say anything, just looked past her, up at the next landing, my footsteps soft, my face friendly, nothing to alert her, nothing for her to worry about, just Joe Citizen pounding up the courthouse stairwell.

On the third step, she passed me, mumbling an insincere 'good day'. In the half-second when I moved past her field of vision, I had the Saran Wrap roll out of the box, pulling out a sheet in the same motion, and then with the speed of a lion, I pounced from behind, wrapping the plastic sheet around her face and pulling back with enough force to jerk her off her feet.

She was so surprised, so disoriented that she couldn't find her feet. In the next few seconds, I had wrapped the roll five times around her head as I continued to pull her backward, up the stairwell, where she would have a hard time gaining any sense of balance. Standing over her shoulder, I could see her eyes roll back, back, back, trying to find my face, trying desperately to make sense of this situation, but she couldn't see who was doing this to her. She flailed with her hands, trying to beat my shoulders, when she should have been trying to dislodge the plastic from her mouth and nose, but I couldn't blame her for putting up a fight, for trying to come to grips with the fact she was being suffocated by a stranger on the dingy steps of the courthouse stairwell, less than fifty feet from the courtroom over which she had presided these last eight years. When she finally stopped struggling and her eyes clouded over, I calmly left the stairwell and headed to the elevator bank. Not a soul stood in the hallway to mark my exit.

# Chapter Six

I am a fraud and a liar. I tell myself I am conditioned, I have discipline, my mind is my possession, an object over which I have control. I tell myself I have the ability to remain in the present, that what separates me from the civilians populating God's green earth is that I, and I alone, can shut off the past like turning off a faucet.

But the damn prostitute in the diner and then this woman who didn't even look like Jake, not really, maybe a little in the eyes, sitting at the table next to me at Augustine's had exposed me for the fraud I am. The faucet had sprung a leak and the leak had caused a flood of memories, but I'll be damned if I wasn't going to plug the miserable thing, right here, right now. I had too much else to worry about.

I am on the road again, heading south now, toward Indianapolis and then Lexington. I am heading out of the blue states toward the red ones, and I know presidential candidate Abe Mann will spend very little time on this part of his whistle-stop tour. He will want to head west quickly, for the key electoral votes represented by Iowa, New Mexico, Nevada, Washington, Oregon, and finally California. But he won't get votes from these states, not a single one from any state, because he will be dead.

I drive like I walk in crowds . . . drawing as little attention to myself as possible: beige rental car, cruise control one-mile-per-hour above the speed limit, blinker whenever I change lanes. I am starting to relax, to wind down, to let my mind drift into a pleasant nothingness, when I spy Pooley out of the corner of my eye, driving a black SUV, a Navigator. He has the passenger window down and is easing alongside me. He signals with one finger, pointed toward the next exit. I immediately slow and allow him to pull in front of me, then follow him to a Shell station just off the Interstate.

'I've got strange news,' he says as we get out and stand next to our cars. He looks tired, like he hasn't slept in days, and his eyelids droop at half-mast.

'You tracked me down, it must be something big.'

'Archibald Grant . . . your middleman who went missing . . .'

'Yeah?'

'I caught up with him at a jailhouse outside of Providence.'

'Jail?'

'Yep. That's what took me so long to locate him. He got pinched on an aiding and abetting racket. Gonna have to serve a few in Federal . . . maybe Lompoc.'

'Shit.'

'Don't worry, he didn't roll on you.'

'You sure?'

'Positive. He knows beyond a shadow of a doubt you can get to him.'

'What about . . .'

'He wouldn't give up who hired him . . . but he said it was someone extremely close to the target.'

'Any hint he knew more than he was letting on? About my history with the mark?'

Pooley shakes his head. 'I don't think so. He's one of these guys who thinks he's a lot more clever than he is . . . you know what I mean? If he knew about your relation to the target, he'd want *me* to know that he knew . . . you see? It'd be a source of pride with him.'

I nod. 'So all we know is that someone close to Mann hired an assassin to kill him.'

'Well, here's where it gets strange, he didn't hire just *one* assassin.'

My eyes flash and Pooley sees it. 'I'm sorry. I didn't know and I know it's my job to know, so go ahead and be pissed . . . I'm sorry. I don't know how I could have missed it . . .'

'Who else is on this job?'

'He wouldn't say.'

'You couldn't coax it out of him.'

'If he hadn't been behind bars, maybe. But it was him and me and a sheet of bulletproof glass twelve inches thick. There was nothing I could do to be persuasive; I had no leverage. I don't think he believes you'll come for him over it.'

'Did you get any indication I might have a head start?'

'He didn't say. He just said the client wanted to make sure the target got clipped and despite your reputation, the client was willing to pay for three guys.'

'Three?' I try to keep my voice even, but I can feel the rising pitch of it in my throat.

Pooley nods. 'Yeah, he hired three guys to finish the job and he doesn't care which one of you completes it. He said the one who does will get the kill fee.'

'Christ.'

'I know.'

'That's two x-factors out there I can't be accountable for, and it only takes one to fuck everything up.'

'I know.'

'Did he tell them all it had to go down in California?'

'Sorry . . . I didn't ask. I'll go back . . .'

'No, fuck that. I need you to find out who the other gunners are . . . as soon as you can.'

Pooley squints in the sunlight, nodding steadily. He

uses his hand as a visor to shield his eyes. 'Yeah, yeah . . . of course. Of course, Columbus.'

'How long will it take you?'

'I don't know. I'll do whatever it takes. A week, tops.'

'Okay. Meet me in Santa Fe in a week with those names. I don't want you to tell me on the phone. Only in person, you understand?'

'Yeah, Columbus. Of course.'

He wants to say more, but he can see in my eyes I'm not in the mood for apologies. So he hops back behind the wheel of the Navigator and pulls out without a backward glance in the mirror.

Bad luck. Bad fucking luck. I feel like ramming the palm of my hand through the steering wheel, but that would be rattling and I don't rattle. One thing I won't do is rattle.

I should turn around and head to the jailhouse outside of Providence, bribe my way in, stick a knife through Archibald Grant's ribs, tell him that's what he gets for hiring three men instead of entrusting the job to one. But he was just doing his client's bidding and if he left out a little information, what does he care? He figures one of us will probably take care of the other two, either before or immediately after the hit, so he'll only have one angry assassin to deal with when it's all said and done. And he figures once that assassin gets paid his kill fee, all apologies will be accepted.

I know I should quit the job, just pull a U-turn at the next exit and head back to Boston, tell Pooley to find me something else, something that doesn't hit quite so close to home. One too many obstacles are stacking up, one too many omens, but for some reason I'm powerless to resist, powerless to put on my blinker and steer this car around, like I'm being pulled by an invisible force, a magnet, something outside of me.

I want to kill my father. I want to be the one to do it, no matter what it takes. The assignment just sped up the inevitable; I was headed on this collision course long before someone paid me. Vespucci said fate causes paths to cross that we cannot understand, but that's not entirely correct. This path I understand perfectly. Abe Mann set me on it a long time ago, the moment he discarded Amanda B. like she was a dead animal he had run over in the street. I am his bastard, and I'll be damned if some other shooter is going to get to him before I do.

I check into the Omni Severin hotel in the middle of downtown Indianapolis. It is one of these large luxury jobs that tries to maintain its historic feel but comes across strangely anachronistic, like it hasn't quite made up its mind what it wants to be, and thus ends up being neither antiquated nor modern.

'I see we have you here for seven days, Mr Smith.'

'Yes.'

'A non-smoking room? King-size bed.'

94

'Yes.'

The clerk, a pretty college student, I would guess, types at her computer. After a moment, she hands me a plastic key-card.

'Now, I should warn you, the final two days of your visit are when Abe Mann will be staying here, and things might get a little . . . you know . . . extra-security and what-not.'

'Really?' I ask, pretending to be pleasantly surprised.

'Yes, sir. Coming through on his "Connecting America" tour or whatever it is he calls it.'

'Are we on the same floor?'

'No . . . he's got the fifteenth floor all to himself. Him and his people, I should say. You won't have to worry about that.'

'Okay, great.' I give her a warm smile. 'That's something, being in Indianapolis at the same time.'

I think that's the reaction she's looking for, and she smiles at me cheerily as she points toward a bank of elevators and gives me directions to my floor.

When I get to my room, I turn on the television and there he is again, as ubiquitous as a celebrity. With twenty-four-hour news channels running at maximum capacity during an election year, I can expect to see candidate Abe Mann any time I flip around the dial. He's standing in front of thirty steel workers, every minority represented, each man dressed in full blue-collar uniform and donning a hard hat. Abe Mann has a hard hat on as well, and he's talking about something he calls a 'Bridge for Working Families', shaking that palm preacher-style, like he genuinely believes what's coming out of his mouth.

The hotel has a pretty good-sized gym, and I decide to pound out my energy on a treadmill. I'm the only one running at this hour; there's a television in the corner showing sports highlights with the sound off, but I ignore it, just pounding my steps in place, settling into a comfortable rhythm, the only noise coming from my steady gait. I plan on running for an hour, and since I am running in place, the past has plenty of time to catch up to me.

I hadn't meant to change, and I was too myopic to understand what was happening to me. Yes, I had killed Mr Cox with a sewing machine in the abandoned Columbus Textile warehouse, but I had loathed Mr Cox, and I had killed him with passion, with emotion, with hatred. When Vespucci opened the door the following morning, I could walk away the same person I was, somehow cleaner, like emerging from a baptism.

But suffocating Judge Janet Stephens with Saran Wrap on the courthouse stairwell was markedly different. It was devoid of emotion, passionless, mechanical, and therefore flawed in a way I could not yet understand. I had done everything right; I had fulfilled my obligation, studied the file, found the weakness, exploited the routine, and my assignment was successful. So what was missing?

I had met Vespucci the next day at a coffee shop at his request.

'You have a bank?' he asked over a small glass cup holding an Americano.

'Yes.'

'Close your account.' He slid me a small sheet of paper. 'Go to this address when you need money. No more records, no more paperwork, no more cheques. Everything will be kept in cash.'

'What will I find at this address?'

'A bank for those of us who don't like banks. You will find you already have an account there. And in that account is fifty thousand dollars that wasn't there yesterday.'

I leaned back, trying to mask that the sum staggered me. Vespucci knew it had, but he didn't say anything more. For a minute, we just sipped our espressos, leaving the air between us silent.

'When do I get my next assignment?' I finally managed.

'When you are ready.'

'I'm ready now.'

'No, Columbus. You need a month to get your . . . how should I say? . . . to get your *edge* back.'

I opened my mouth, but then closed it while his eyes measured me. He was right. I wasn't ready. Though I couldn't put my finger on what was holding me back.

'This business, this business you find yourself in, it pays well but it also exacts a fee, Columbus. Do I make sense? It exacts a fee up here . . .' He tapped his head with his index finger. 'The only currency by which you can pay this fee is time. You need some time so you can do what you do again.'

I nodded, but I knew he had more.

'I think it is not enough to do your job and walk away from it. I believe . . . this is hard to understand . . . I believe you must connect with your mark's mind . . . ahhh . . .' He waved off his words as though he were displeased with them, like they had failed to communicate what he was trying to say. I waited. After a moment, he spread his hands in front of him. 'Columbus, I did not give you enough lead time because it was a test to see how you would do. Typically, you will have eight weeks before an assignment must be complete. Use the time to not only know the routine of your mark, but to know what is going on inside your mark's head, to become your mark, to really understand his . . . or her . . . motivations. Once you have fully *realized* the connection, only then can you fully *sever* the connection. Do not ask me to explain why this is so. I only know it is.'

With that, he dropped a ten-spot on the table to cover our bill, excused himself, and shuffled out of the coffee house.

★    ★    ★

Jake could tell I had changed. She didn't know how to ask what was different about me, why I was acting morose, so she grew frustrated.

'What did I do?' We were sitting down to dinner.

'You didn't do anything.'

'Ever since we came back from New Hampshire you've been acting . . . I don't know . . . *bothered* by me.'

'I'm telling you this has nothing to do with you, Jake.'

'Bullshit.'

'What do you want me to say? You need to drop it.' I could feel my anger rising like boiled water.

This was our first row and I discovered she wasn't one to back down. 'Drop what? How can I drop something when you won't even tell me what I'm supposed to be dropping?'

I started to answer but she interrupted, 'I'd expect this from some people, but not you. Since the day I met you, we've been nothing but honest with each other. That's what having a relationship, a real relationship, is all about. You have to trust me and I have to trust you. There isn't any other way to do it – not a way that works, that really works.'

She was right, but my hands were tied. 'You're right, I'm sorry.'

I could see her eyes soften, but she held firm. 'You're apologizing but I don't even know what you're apologizing for. This isn't communicating. This is me talking to a brick wall.'

'I said I'm sorry, Jake. I'm trying to figure some things out, but you have to believe that the problems I'm having aren't about us. The *only* thing . . . the only thing I depend on each day *is* us. I know that's not a satisfying answer but I need you to accept it . . . I'll get down and beg you to accept it if that's what it takes. But I can't handle you going sour on me too. I just . . . can't. When the time is right, I'll tell you everything.'

Whatever defenses she had melted away. 'You promise?' she said, weakly.

'I promise.'

'You trust me? Completely?'

'You're the only one I do trust on this planet.'

'I love you.'

When I answered her with the same three words, I meant them fully.

# Chapter Seven

My next assignment was a disaster. The name on the top of the page was Richard Levine, a numbers runner on the east side. Vespucci had done his homework, but even the homework had gaping holes in it, gaping holes due to a very specific reason: I was working a job where the target knew I was coming.

Levine was a five-foot-two slight figure with chronic headaches and a short fuse. He had made a fortune working the rackets among the union workers down by Boston Harbor, and as his bank account increased, so did the list of his enemies. A cautious man, he had a regular staff of five bodyguards . . . professional guys, former cops, men who hadn't had a chance to go soft. He lived in a large house near Beacon Hill and rarely went out any more, letting his minions work the books, deliver the payouts, and make the collections. A handful of guys were entrusted to enter his door, and all of these guys were known faces, fellas who had been on his payroll for ten-plus years. None of these men left the business either; the only way to get away from Levine was to die or disappear.

Vespucci didn't have schematics on the inside of his house; they had mysteriously vanished from the Department of Records downtown. My fence also knew better than to talk to any of Levine's men. I had eight weeks and very little information. But it was the last sentence in the file that got my attention: *'Mark knows he has a price tag on his head.'*

The son-of-a-bitch knew, knew someone had been hired to kill him, knew bullets were being loaded into cylinders at this very moment, intended to strike him dead.

What I had to do, what Vespucci inherently knew I must do, was to get inside the head of my mark, *realize* the connection so I could *sever* the connection, as he said. But how could I crack Levine if I couldn't get close to him?

I started by jogging down his street wearing a Boston College T-shirt and some athletic shorts I'd purchased from a bookstore close to the school. I'm sure I looked like every other out-of-breath runner, cutting through neighbourhoods near the park to break a sweat and get the ol' heart rate up.

His street was common, lined with expensive homes, the stand-out feature being Levine's house at the end of the block. Gated, with an expansive lawn, it was a two-storey Tudor mansion looking down on the rest of the homes like a pedantic school-teacher in front of a classroom. I didn't stop to tie a shoelace and get more of a look; it was too early in the game to raise any eyebrows.

From the file Vespucci gave me, I pulled out a chart with the names and faces of Levine's pigeons, the low-level guys who handled the sports books around town. Vespucci had also included the name of a bar in Little Italy where a couple of the guys liked to whittle away time instead of going home to their wives. It wasn't much, but it was a start.

I eased into Antonio's on Stuart Street, just down from Maggiano's. It was a small place, dimly lit, with a long oak bar covering the length of the back wall. A couple of dartboards, a jukebox, three tables, a tele-vision tuned in to the Sox, and a fat Irishman pouring drinks for an eclectic crowd of locals, college kids, and tourists.

Two of Levine's bookies were at a table near the box, drinking beer and watching the game through jaded eyes. I tried to pick up snippets of conversation, but most of it revolved around the fuckin' Sox this and the fuckin' Sox that.

I watched the final out as the Boston cleanup hitter grounded weakly to the pitcher. 'Fuck!' I said loudly, and followed it with, 'that cost me a grand.' I didn't have to turn around to know my words had found their mark. As I downed the last of my beer, I heard chairs scraping over the wooden floor, then heavy footsteps, and finally two sets of eyeballs appeared on either side of me.

'You bet the Sox, kid?'

I turned around with a frown on my face, and made eye contact with the shorter of the two guys, the one I knew was named Ponts.

'Yeah. Shit. I know you should never bet your heart . . . but I had a *feeling* tonight.'

Ponts snorted. 'Happens to all of us.'

The taller of the two, a bookie who I knew was named Gorti, jumped in with . . . 'shit, don't it?'

'What you drinking, kid?' Ponts asked.

'Me?' I looked at the bottle like I didn't know. 'Budweiser.'

Ponts called out to the bartender. 'Three Buds, Seamus . . .'

'You don't have to—'

'Christ, you just lost a grand on the goddamn Sox. It's the least I could do.'

The beers appeared in front of us in a hurry. 'Thanks, then . . .' I said.

'Who you bet with, kid?'

I pulled down the bottle from my mouth and looked at Ponts suspiciously.

'Bet with?'

'Who's your bookmaker?'

'You guys cops?'

They looked at each other and started chuckling. 'Nah, kid. We ain't cops.'

'We are *far* from cops, I can guarantee you that,' added Gorti.

'Well, just the same . . . thanks for the beer. But I should—'

Ponts didn't let me finish the sentence, 'Kid, the reason I'm asking is because Ben Gorti here and me, Stu Ponts, Ben and me run book right out of this bar.'

'Oh, yeah?' I tried to look pleasantly surprised.

'That's right. And lemme guess, you're still using your daddy's bookie somewhere back wherever home is?'

I let out a smile like he was right on the money.

'Well, what d'ya say you let your old man run his own game and you start running one with us?'

'Really, I should—'

'Tell you what . . . what's your typical lay?'

'How much you bet, kid?' added Gorti, as if to clarify.

'I usually go five hundred. Unless I'm feeling it. Then, who knows . . .' I tried to sound like a fish who had just bitten on the worm and gotten the hook.

Ponts's grin widened. 'Well, I'll give you your first $500 bet on the house, and a five-thousand-dollar credit line. Does your dad's bookie give you that?'

'No, sir.'

'Call me Ponts.'

'Okay . . .'

He clasped me on the back with a beefy hand. 'Now, who you like this week in the Miami game?'

There is a common misconception following a successful assassination. Often, the people closest to the target will say they never got a look at the hired killer, they don't know how the assassin could have gotten close to their boss; the man came in like a ghost and put a bullet in their friend, husband, co-worker without disturbing the dust in the air. They'll say someone in their midst must have betrayed him, they'll look at each other with skeptical eyes, they'll check over their shoulders every time a shadow moves across a doorway, every time they cross in front of a dark alley.

But the truth is they've often known the face of the trigger man, they've probably shaken hands with him, probably done business with him, hell, probably bought him a beer in a small sports bar in Little Italy.

If I couldn't know Levine, if I couldn't make a connection with him, I could watch his pigeons, I could get to know his roots, where he came from before he lived in the big house on the hill at the end of the street. He got to where he was by being the best at what Ponts and Gorti did now. My guess is he was more ruthless, less forgiving then the typical runner. I didn't know if he demanded the same of his employees, but I intended to find out.

★   ★   ★

It didn't all go wrong on the day of the hit; it happened the night before I pulled the trigger. I was into the guys for most of my nut, the initial amount of credit they gave me to hook me. I played stupidly right off the bat; I didn't have time to make casual bets. I started with sucker plays, parlays, rolling any wins I stumbled upon, pushing the limits, and Ponts lapped it up like a stray cat with a fresh bottle of milk. In three weeks, I flopped on enough games to be into the fat man for forty-eight hundred.

I met up with him as he was coming out of Antonio's.

'Say, kid . . .'

'Hey, Ponts. Can I get on a parlay this weekend?'

'How much?'

'Double up, catch up.'

He let out a low whistle. 'Forty-eight?'

'Might as well make it an even five.'

'What say you give me the forty-eight you already owe, and we'll go from there?'

'Come on, Ponts . . . you said a five-grand credit line.'

'But, kid—'

'Forty-eight is not five.'

'Yeah, but you want to go in for ten—'

'Not if I win—'

'I don't know, kid.'

'Fine . . . I'll just put two hundred on a three-way parlay . . . B.C. getting three, the over, and Virginia Tech over Michigan.'

'You just want two hundred?'

'I want five dimes, but you said you'll only give me two potatoes.'

He looked at me sideways and pulled out a small notepad. 'The kid wants five dimes . . . I'll give the kid five dimes. Five to win fifteen on the parlay. Let's just hope your luck turns, buddy.'

'I got a feeling this time.'

He smiled and winked. 'I hope so.'

I hit the B.C. game but lost both Tech and the over. Now, I owed Ponts and Gorti ninety-eight hundred and I would get my first impression of how they ticked when wound up. I stayed away from Antonio's for two weeks, just to get their engines into the red. Maybe they thought I'd run out on them. Maybe they thought I wasn't coming back.

When I showed up at the bar, Ponts's mouth disappeared into a thin line. All hints of camaraderie and companionship were gone. I was not his friend; this was business.

'Where's the ninety-eight hundred?' he said as I sidled up to the bar. Gorti took a position on the other side of me.

'Let me finish my beer.' I was playing the spoiled college kid for all it was worth.

Ponts took the beer bottle out of my hand and downed it in front of me in two quick gulps. 'Now you're finished. Where's my money?'

I pulled out a roll of bills from my pocket. 'I got five large here. If you'll just let me place it on tonight's game . . .'

The fat man snatched it out of my hand, quickly handed it to Gorti, who began to thumb through it. After a quick count, he nodded back to Ponts.

'You got five days to come up with the other forty-eight.'

'Come on . . . why so hostile . . . ?'

'You think this is hostile? Hostile is Friday morning if you don't have my money.'

'Jesus. I went out of town for a few days. Here I am and I paid you.'

'You paid me half.'

'I don't see why . . .'

And then my voice trailed off, the words choking in my throat. The last thing I was expecting, and the very thing Vespucci had warned me about, rose up and stung me.

Jake walked into the bar with a friend of hers.

Now, my plan had been to show up on Friday and ask for an extension, to claim poor, to see how physical Ponts would get with me when I didn't have the money. I was beginning to understand why Vespucci preached making a connection with the target; it was my job to seek out the *evil* in people. Everyone has a dark side, and once I find that dark side, it is my job to home in on it, manipulate it, exploit it, enlarge it. I must see the evil in the target, taste it, put my finger in it the way Thomas did to the wound of Christ, so that the act of killing becomes diminished, becomes necessary. It is a trick of sorts, an illusion created by the mind to keep the horrors of the job at bay. I wanted to see what Ponts would do to me, so that when I killed Levine, I would understand what he had done to others. Then I could walk away from it like a vigilante instead of a hired gun, at peace with my decision to take someone's life.

But all that changed the moment Jake walked into the bar and saw me.

She immediately dove-tailed over to where I was standing and kissed my lips, saying my name . . . a different name than what I had given Ponts and Gorti.

I started to say something to get her to walk away, but Ponts read me like a book and interrupted before any words could come out of my mouth, addressing Jake directly.

'Hello, there! I'm Ponts and this is Gorti . . . we're friends of your boyfriend. What's your name, beautiful?'

She turned to them warmly. 'Jake. Jake Owens.'

Ponts grinned so large I thought he was going to swallow her. 'You go to school here, Jake Owens?'

She nodded. 'Almost finished at B.C. How do you boys know each other?'

'We're old friends from way back, aren't we?' and he said my name, the one Jake had handed to him.

'Yeah,' I mumbled. 'You know, Jake . . . let me finish up with these fellas and I'll come sit with you.'

'Okay,' she said, like she knew she had interrupted something she shouldn't have.

'It was nice meeting you, Jake Owens from B.C.' Ponts said, holding the words like he didn't want to let them go.

As soon as she was gone, his eyes hardened. 'I don't care you gave us a bum name, I don't care you think you're so fucking smart you can game us like a couple of fruits. What I do care about is the forty-eight big you owe us. Now you know that we know about Jake Owens from B.C. We get the money on Friday or somebody's day gets ruined. We understand each other?'

I nodded. 'Yeah . . . sure, Ponts.'

'Don't do anything dumb again, kid.' He patted the side of my face and turned back to the bar like the conversation was over.

I was sweating. I sat in my apartment, the window open, a nice breeze blowing in off the water, and yet I was sweating, like the room had nothing but stale air trapped inside.

I had ignored Vespucci's advice, I had kept up my relationship with a girl who loved me, and now she was involved. Two low-level bag men for my primary target knew her name and even worse . . . knew mine.

I was going to have to rectify the situation. Rectify it myself, without telling Vespucci what I planned. And

I felt it had to be as soon as possible, money or no money. I didn't know what Ponts and Gorti would do to warn me, to send me a message even before Friday's deadline, so I had to compress my six weeks into that moment.

I sat in the shadows of a neighbouring stoop, watching the front door of Antonio's. An intermittent rain was falling, and drops pooled on the lid of my black baseball cap before collecting into a puddle at my feet. My eyes were sharp, hard, focused. I waited, ignoring everything but the front door of the restaurant, not even stamping my feet to shake off the chill wind blowing in from the east.

At midnight, Ponts and Gorti shuffled out of the bar. They weren't stumbling; I'd noticed neither man ever drank more than a couple of beers the whole time they were at Antonio's. They wanted to look like they were there to have a good time, but Antonio's was a job to them, as mundane as any cubicle at any office in America. So when they left the bar, they were both sober.

From casing them over the last couple of weeks, I knew they both rode together in a four-door Oldsmobile, the kind of car only the elderly and ex-cons purchase with any regularity. As soon as they both settled into the front seat, I flipped open the rear door and slid in behind them.

They both spun to get a look at me, surprised.

'What'ya doin', kid?' Gorti asked, a moment before

I shot him through the passenger seat. He gasped for air – the bullet shattered his left lung – but I was no longer concerned with him, I just turned the gun on Ponts, who was hunched uncomfortably behind the steering wheel, breathing raspily.

'Jesus fuckin' Christ, kid, don't shoot me.'

'Just drive.'

'I got a wife at home—'

'I said drive.'

'Sure, kid. Sure.'

He turned on the ignition and put the car into gear, then slowly pulled it out onto the street. Little Italy was dark and empty at this time of night, the cold and the rain keeping the pedestrians at bay.

'Take the highway south. I'll tell you when to get off.'

Ponts tried to make small talk along the way. Told me it was only five grand and he could chalk that up to sour business. Told me his wife was talking about finally having a baby this year. Told me he didn't even remember my girlfriend's name if that was what this was about.

I let him talk as much as he wanted, until he finally gave up and drove the car in silence. I stayed out of his sight-line in the rearview mirror, allowing the danger to expand like noxious fumes in his mind. He didn't know where the gun was, where my eyes were, when the shot might come.

I gave him a few directions until we ended up outside the abandoned Columbus Textile Warehouse, where I had last taken Pete Cox's life and emerged, like a phoenix, with a new one of my own.

Inside, the warehouse was much as I had last seen it. No police tape, no evidence bags, no fingerprint dust. Cox's body and any sign of foul play had been meticulously erased by Vespucci's men.

I directed Ponts to a chair at an old sewing desk. His legs were shaky, but he managed to make it this far without passing out, even if his breathing grew progressively more laboured, like a dog's pant after a hard run.

'What we doin' here, Columbus?'

So it was back to the name I had given him originally; that was a good sign. I pulled out some paper and a pencil I had tucked away in my pocket before I left my apartment.

'You're going to draw me a map.'

He started to say something but then just waited for me to continue. 'I want an exact layout of Richard Levine's house: bedrooms, living room, kitchen, shitters, laundry room, where he eats, where he sleeps, where he takes a dump. I want X's marking where his guards sit, where they head when they take their breaks, where they come in, where they go out. I want you to write down every detail you can think of about that house and all the people in it.'

'Fuck. You're the guy. The hired gun.' He looked up at me in awe, like I had just pulled the greatest magic trick of all time right in front of him.

I let my eyes go hard in answer. 'Start writing.'

It was about an hour to daylight when Ponts and I started walking up the front porch of Levine's house. I knew cameras were covering us, but I had a gun in his ribs and my ball cap pulled down tight over my head. Knowing where the cameras were positioned helped me keep my face off the security screens. And I knew we were coming about twenty minutes before the guards changed shifts. There is no man who isn't tired at 5:30 A.M., especially when he knows he's heading to a warm bed after a long, boring, rainy night.

We arrived at the front door, and Ponts rang the bell. An intercom affixed to a support column on the patio barked to life.

'What you doin' here, Ponts?'

'I got a favour to ask of Dick.'

'Come back after breakfast.'

'This can't wait, Ernie. This is my sister's kid I got with me. He works first shift on the docks, but he's looking for some fries on the side. I already told Dick about it; I know he's up reading the *Daily Racing Form* . . . come on, we'll be in and out.'

'Levine knows *you're* coming?'

'I mentioned it to him a couple weeks ago. He said he'd work it in 'cause it was me.'

Despite the fact that I had told him he would live through this if he just played his part to the end, the last sound Ponts ever heard was the door clicking open. He had served his purpose, and I didn't want to put off shooting him.

The whole thing took eight minutes. I pulled the trigger on Ponts and kicked the door back at the same time, smashing it into the first guard who was coming to frisk me. As he fell backwards, I shot him in the head, sending the back of his skull into a potted begonia in the foyer. The silencer attached to the pistol's muzzle kept the report from sounding like anything more than a small cough.

I didn't care about the dining room to the right, so I stepped left and shot the two guards seated around the kitchen table before they could even get their guns up. Two chest shots, and their blood poured into their blue starched shirts, a pair of purple ovals where their front pockets used to be.

Without breaking stride, I moved up the back stairwell, my legs like pistons as I attacked each step, moving quickly now, reloading my pistols as I went. First, I shot the guard sitting sleepy-eyed on a stool at the top of the staircase reading his *USA TODAY*, a face shot, so that all of his features became an indistinguishable red mask. Another guard emerged from a bathroom, a fat guy, an extra guy, the one Ponts hadn't told me about. I figured there would be some sort of play Ponts would try to make, a last piece of information he would hold for himself, so he could wait and use it when I would be surprised, vulnerable. But Ponts was dead and this poor player had the misfortune of taking his end-of-shift shit right as I was coming up the stairs. He didn't have time to exhale before I shot him in the heart.

The last guy left was Richard Levine, the one-time numbers runner and current bookmaking heavy of Boston, Massachusetts. And I hated him. Not because of his operation, or his business, or the evil I could imagine he must have harnessed to rise to the level he had.

No, I hated him because of what this assignment meant, what it uncovered, what it cost me. Vespucci was right all along. I couldn't go back to Jake, not now, not ever again. If I couldn't account for her whereabouts at all times, if I couldn't keep her behind locked doors, if I couldn't protect her from my world, then she would always be in play, always be a factor, always be involved in a race she didn't know she was running. And for all that, I loathed Richard Levine with every living cell in my body.

When I entered his bedroom, he was seated on a back patio, drinking orange juice and reading the *Racing Form*. He turned his head and his eyes met mine and he instantly knew my purpose, why I was there, what I was going to do with the weapon in my hand. For a moment, just a moment, his eyes dropped, like he was resigned this day would come, the race he was running had reached the finish line. And then as quickly as it was there, it was gone again, replaced by the steel and spit and resolve that had driven him the last twenty years. He leapt for the nearest chair cushion, knocking the table up and out of the way, sending his breakfast dishes flying in what he hoped was the distraction he needed to reach the gun tucked underneath the nearest wicker chair.

My first bullet caught him just below his arm, breaking his ribs and sapping the fight out of him the way a strong body blow can shut down even the toughest of heavyweights. It spun him, so that he wheeled into the overturned table and dropped into the mess of food and juice and shattered glass on the floor. The chair he was trying to reach spilled over in his fall, and the gun it harboured tumbled out just a few feet from where his body came to rest. He looked at the gun the way a covetous man looks at his neighbour's wife, so close, yet a mile away. I'm sure he was thinking, 'if only I'd been a little faster'.

My second bullet stopped him from thinking, permanently.

# Chapter Eight

I am watching Abe Mann at a rally in downtown Indianapolis. He is standing on a podium, with a hundred fidgeting children on risers behind him, talking about building a foundation of learning in this country, talking about accountability and responsibility and private school credits and tax breaks for working families. Empty words told by rote with little feeling, like he's starting to sag under the weight of a hundred campaign speeches to a hundred sleepy-eyed crowds, with no end in sight.

I am one of those sleepy-eyed crowd members, though my half-closed lids are an act, a mask, a shield I can hide behind while my eyes seek out and record every detail of the event. There are four teachers on either side of the risers, wearing green and gold 'James A. Garfield Elementary School' T-shirts, two black women and two white males. The men are so obviously members of the Secret Service their presence is more warning than undercover work; they are dressed that way so the pictures in tomorrow's *Indianapolis Star* will not project a leader who needs constant protection.

A row of photographers stands at the front of the crowd in a small section marked by steel dividers. There are several goateed men, most with ponytails, and only a few women, snapping pictures between yawns, just doing their jobs. Any one of them could kill Abe Mann rather easily and at close range, but getting away would pose a problem. The kill is only half of the assignment; disappearing after the body drops is where an assassin earns his fee.

I would guess the crowd stands about five hundred strong, and I am dressed like most of the young men here: grey business suit, dark tie, black shoes, and black belt. Normally, I would have worn sunglasses, but the sky is overcast, and I do not want to draw any unnecessary attention my way. As I've said, there is a way of standing, of dressing, of combing your hair, of holding a blank expression on your face, of folding your hands, of yawning when someone looks your way that renders you all but invisible in a crowd, a room, even tight quarters, like a hallway.

I count eight Secret Service men mingling in the audience, conspicuous by the slight bulges under their arms that shoulder holsters make in clothing, and by the number of times they look around the crowd instead of keeping their eyes on the speaker. I can guess their ranks will swell as we move further west and closer to the convention. How many of them I will eventually have to negotiate is still to be discovered.

I wait until the speech is over and the audience disperses *en masse*. Although dozens of supporters trickled away before the event reached its conclusion, I find I can be more inconspicuous if I remain a sheep in the flock instead of a straggler. I catch one last glimpse of candidate Mann as he clasps hands with various attendees while leaving the podium. His face is fatigued, and although he is grinning, there is melancholy in his eyes.

From Indianapolis, the Mann tour heads to Little Rock, Oklahoma City, and Santa Fe. I follow, but I do not attend another rally, nor do I check into the same hotel as Mann and his entourage. But I do stand in front of the television and parrot the words of his speeches over and over until I have the lines memorized. I begin to understand how little of a political stump speech is improvised. He'll add a joke with local flavour to the beginning of each speech, something to let the crowd know he's interested in their city, their state, their problems. Then he'll transition into the same lines he's already used a thousand times. I understand his ennui. It is damn near impossible to bring passion to weightless words.

When I reach Santa Fe, I head for the La Fonda, a pueblo-style Spanish hotel on the plaza. A sign above the door indicates it is 'the Inn at the End of the Trail', but that is a lie. The trail isn't anywhere near its end, not for me. I check in and wait for a knock on my door.

Pooley arrives three hours later. I have taken the opportunity to work in a light nap, and I feel refreshed when he steps into the room. He is holding a thick manila envelope. His expression is sober.

'What'd you find out?' I say once we ask after each other's health.

'One piece of the puzzle. They definitely hired two other assassins for this job besides you. Shooter number two is a Spanish contract killer named Miguel Cortega. He worked a little out of New York and Chicago before he made his way to D.C. Who knows what he did before crossing the Atlantic.'

'You familiar with him?'

Pooley shakes his head. 'I went through some back channels to pull the name, called in a chit I had with William Ryan out of Vegas. He made some calls and gave up Cortega.'

Ryan was a high-level West Coast fence who repped both sides: acquirers and killers. Pooley and I had worked with him once before and were both impressed with his professionalism.

'Had Ryan used him before?'

'Twice. Both long-range sniper shots and both confirmed kills.'

'A drop man.'

Pooley nods. 'Looks like it.'

'Does Cortega know he's been tripled, or is he in the dark like I was?'

'I told Ryan to tread lightly. He can't be sure, but he thinks he's running blind right now.'

'Does he know if Cortega has a kill date, or is he going to make a move upon opportunity?'

'The assignment is to drop the candidate the week of the convention, same as you.'

I let out a deep breath. 'Well, that's good at least. He's a pro, so he won't jump the gate early. Which means I still have some time to set the table.'

'Maybe. Maybe not.'

'Go on.'

'Shooter number three. I don't have a name, but I know who his fence is.'

'Who?'

'You're not going to like it.'

'Who is it, Pooley? Jesus.'

'Vespucci.'

I looked at my friend long and hard as that name engulfed me like a poisonous cloud. I hadn't heard it out loud in so long, I had sometimes wondered if that dark Italian was still in the game. I guess he is, and some strange part of me feels . . . what is it . . . pride? Pride that I have a chance to prove myself to that old bastard again? Pride that I will take out one of his men and complete the assignment out from under him?

Pride that he will have to face the fact I am still alive? Or am I confused and the emotion I feel, for the first time in a long time, is fear?

Pooley coughs into his hand. 'I know his name brings yet another personal connection into this mission, but I think it's better you have all the cards in front of you.'

'Of course it is.' I snap out of my reverie and meet Pooley's eyes to let him know I'm back, focused. 'But you don't know who he put on the job?'

'I tried to get the information but I met a brick wall. I don't know what power that old Italian wields, but he has a lot of tongues afraid to wag.'

'Okay, good work, Pooley.'

He smiles. 'This assignment sure is stirring up some echoes.'

'Yeah.'

'There're plenty of other jobs out there. You can drop off and we wouldn't miss a beat.'

I shake my head. 'This one's mine, Pooley. And there's a reason it's mine, even if that reason is a little grey right now.'

'You're getting philosophical on me.'

'Maybe.'

'Well, I'll leave you to your ramblings then,' he says with a smirk.

'Can you do a couple of things for me before you head back to Boston?'

'Anything.'

'I want a new car, an SUV, something bigger.'

'Done.'

'And I want you to stop by Mann's local head-quarters. Tell 'em you're a contractor, you handle special events all over the country. See what kind of process they have for securing bids on Mann events. See if they use a local or a national company. Someone puts up the risers, someone coordinates the kids and the construction workers and the cops and the soldiers to stand behind him. I want to know who and how they get the job.'

'You got it. It'll probably be late tomorrow, Friday at the latest.'

'Do what you got to do. Take the spare key on the dresser. I'll stay here until I see you again.'

He starts to leave, then stops, and turns to face me, holding up that envelope. 'I almost forgot. Here.'

'What's this?'

'Some more research I pulled. Don't ask me how. It's a . . . what's the word . . . addendum to the initial material. I think it'll help you focus.'

'Why do you say I need focus?'

'It's in your eyes, Columbus.'


I am sitting in a booth in McDonald's, the most American of fast-food restaurants. I read recently that Abe Mann likes to eat quarter-pounders here, a page he stole from Bill Clinton's playbook. By eating greasy burgers at a popular fast-food chain, he can give off the impression he is 'one of us', a true 'man of the people', not some stuffy aristocrat who sits for five-hundred-dollar haircuts and windsurfs on the waves outside his mansion in Nantucket. His handlers are playing their cards deftly; Mann's numbers continue to rise in the polls and his press has been favourable. He is on auto-pilot, careful not to make a mistake this close to the convention, not with his nomination at stake, and so his campaign is as lifeless as the burger on the tray in front of me. We are both on missions, headed for the same spot on the map.

A brown dog is loitering in the parking lot outside the window. He doesn't appear to belong to anyone, at least not any more, and he is skittish, like he's taken too many kicks to the ribs and isn't going to let it happen again. He is sniffing by the dumpsters across the lot, but whatever he's looking for, he doesn't find it.

I open the envelope Pooley handed me and slide out a stack of papers. It's another jigsaw puzzle, only this one is already put together, all the pieces lined up and fitted in place. Newspaper clippings and hotel receipts and bank statements and official testimony and diary entries, all presented succinctly and chronologically to tell a complete story. How Pooley put this together, or, more likely, who gave it to him, are questions for which I'm not sure I want the answers. It turns out my mother, LaWanda Dickerson, isn't the only woman Abe Mann removed permanently from his life.

Her name was Nichelle Spellman. She was a senior vice-president of regional planning for Captain-McGuire-Magness, a worldwide agriculture processor headquartered in Topeka, Kansas. She met Abe Mann for the first time when she spoke in front of a congressional committee formed to explore allegations of price-fixing amongst the farming conglomerates. Over an eight-year period, they met frequently, and secretly, at various functions all over the world.

Nichelle Spellman had a husband of eleven years and a seven-year-old daughter. She was moderately pretty, a little plump, with dark eyes and dark hair. She was a bit Midwestern plain, but had an Ivy League education and a gift for making people feel comfortable. In her capacity as a senior VP for CMM, she also had a boatload of bribery money.

She had started off with small purchases, pushing the envelope on what congressmen could take as 'gifts': tickets to Vegas shows, celebrity golf Pro-Ams, items that drew raised eyebrows from the ethics committee but no inquiries. Mann grew adept at hiding money, using middlemen, opening accounts all over the world. For years, the relationship grew until the amount of money exchanging hands became staggering. In return, Congress stayed out of CMM's affairs. Special committees dissolved. Allegations dropped. Price-fixing in agriculture didn't have the same sizzle as steroids in Major League baseball or obscenities in Hollywood, and so it wasn't difficult to turn a blind eye. A blind eye that came with a seven-figure price tag.

The relationship ended abruptly when the FBI snatched up Nichelle Spellman in a bribery sting. Mann was not aware of the Bureau's actions until after the fact. He tried to contact her on eleven separate occasions, but his calls went unanswered, unreturned. He needed her to remain silent. He needed to know she would take the fall, his name wouldn't come up, not when he had just been elected Speaker of the House. The FBI continued to build their case and there was talk of a Grand Jury, of testimony, of things being said 'on the record'.

On May 16 of that year, a week before the Grand Jury would hear Ms Spellman's testimony, Nichelle's daughter Sadie was abducted directly out of her classroom. A man entered the school, telling the teacher he was from Nichelle's husband's office and Sadie needed to come with him right away. There was an emergency. The man seemed confident, articulate and unthreatening, and the teacher complied without hesitation. A week later, Nichelle pleaded the Fifth to every question the Grand Jury asked her. She was distraught but resolute; she was asked if she needed more time in light of her family's personal tragedy and she said no, this was her testimony, this was what she wanted on the record. The Grand Jury was stymied. Abe Mann's name never passed her lips.

One month later, an undercover Kansas police officer, along with Nichelle, her husband, and her daughter were all found dead in a snowy ditch near an abandoned airfield, shot at close range multiple times. The newspapers described it as a botched kidnapping hand-off, a sorry ending to a sad affair. The daughter's body had shown signs of assault. No suspect was ever arrested.

I put down the papers, turning the new information over in my mind.

It seems Abe Mann has grown comfortable ordering the deaths of people. Nichelle hadn't even talked, hadn't given him up, and he still wanted the loose ends tied, wanted the coffin lids closed so no one would have a change of heart or a wandering tongue at a later date.

How many times had he ordered executions besides the two I know of? How many bodies are buried deep in his congressional closet? Does he take pleasure from it, acting as God, acting as one who decides between life and death?

It seems I am more like my father than I thought.

At a table a few feet away, a man is eating by himself, obviously waiting on someone. His feet tap the floor nervously, and his eyes flit to the door every few seconds. Eventually, a harried woman comes in, two small boys in tow. I keep my head buried in the file, chewing methodically on my quarter-pounder, trying not to look up, even as the couple barks at each other.

'We said twelve-thirty. I've been here an hour.'

'You try packing up all their shit for a weekend with no help. None!'

'I tried calling your cell phone.'

'Well, maybe I was a little busy, did you ever think of that?'

'Well, maybe I'll bring them back an hour late on Monday.'

'Don't do me any favours.'

'Real nice, Amy. Real nice. Right in front of 'em.'

'Oh, don't you dare get self-righteous with me . . .'

After a few more exchanges, the woman storms out, leaving the father alone with the two boys. Each of them carries a backpack, and, on their faces, shame.

I finish my lunch and take the tray to the trashcan, dumping the contents and pushing the tray onto the shelf. The grease is still on my tongue, and even as I suck my large soda dry, it remains there, resistant and defiant.

When I step into the parking lot, it is impossible to avoid the small crowd gathered in a half-circle near my rental car. I don't want to meet any eyes, I just want to get to my car and drive away, but it is too late for that. They are looking at me, shaking their heads, wanting me to join in, wanting me to see what they see and feel the misery they feel.

The woman who dropped off her kids has stepped out of her minivan, but left the driver's door open, the engine idling.

'I didn't see it. It just darted in front of me.'

The brown dog lies on the ground in front of her van, his back legs broken, his eyes wild. He tries to get to his front feet but can't, and so lies back down, breathing rapidly, mustering the strength to try again, repeating the cycle over and over.

Try, fail, rest, try, fail, rest. Try. Fail.

I make my way past the courtyard of the La Fonda, past businessmen and women finishing their lunches, and head for the ground-floor hallway, the corridor to my room.

Then the world slows, the sound drops out, everything fades to a single image, like looking through a tunnel toward the light at the other end. A single image, as in-focus as anything I've ever seen in my life. A man is coming out of my room, a gun in his hand, backing out, fresh blood on his face, and his eyes meet mine. I recognize him, I *know* him. I haven't seen him in years, but I know him all right. I loaded his beer-truck, he introduced me to the dark Italian, he brought Cox into that textile mill. I always knew that he, Hap Blowenfeld, was a killer, that he had been recruited by Vespucci before me, that the beer-truck job must have been a cover for an assignment; and in that moment, that crystal clear moment in which we were seeing each other, I took in every detail about *this* Hap, the one in the present, the one carrying a brand new Beretta, the one who still weighs roughly a hundred and ninety pounds, the one who has a three-inch scar on his forehead that wasn't there before, the one who has Pooley's blood on his face.

And then, wham, everything speeds back to normal though it is all heightened, the colours somehow crisper, the smells stronger, and Hap doesn't hesitate. He levels his gun at me and fires a silenced bullet, but I am moving fast now like a leopard that has spotted a predator in the jungle bigger than he. I dart back toward the courtyard as the bullet slams into the wall just inches behind my head, and I know Hap won't follow me, he has been trained like me to blend in, but that isn't my concern, my concern is to walk as quickly and as normally as I can back through the lobby and out to my car, the Range Rover Pooley had waiting for me in the parking lot of the INN AT THE END OF THE TRAIL this morning, and maybe, just maybe I will not draw any stares, and maybe, just maybe I can spot that bastard driving off before he gets away clean.

I throw the car into gear and race around the building just in time to see a black Audi exiting onto San Francisco street, tyres squealing as it passes from concrete to asphalt. Yes, finally, one fucking good thing in this terrible day, between that dog, that fucking dog with two broken legs trying to get to its feet after it careened off the front bumper of that haggard mother's mini-van and fucking Pooley, sticking around in Santa Fe when he should have been heading back East, but I told him to stay because I wanted more goddamn information, information I could have gotten myself, and I brought him into this life and because of me he's dead, poor fucking Pooley, dealt the worst fucking hands all his goddamn life.

I didn't have to see his body to know what had happened: Vespucci was a good fence and he had sniffed out the multiple assassins hired for this job and Hap had spotted me on Mann's trail because he would have been doing the same thing I was doing, trying to get inside the candidate's head, *make* the connection so he could *sever* the connection. And so he had seen me, and staked me, and he went into that room thinking it was me in there, but Pooley was waiting for me, and so got a bullet in his head when the door opened. If it wasn't that, then it was a version pretty damn close to that, and now Hap was widening the distance between us because he was in an Audi and I had cavalierly told Pooley to get me something bigger, an SUV, thinking I had all the time in the world to make my plans.

An hour passes before I realize the Audi is gone, and I am alone.

# Chapter Nine

Darkness. Black darkness.

And pain.

I have checked into a nondescript hotel, and I am sitting on the bed in the darkness, listening to the occasional rumble of the big rigs as they make their way down Highway 84, and I am thinking.

Earlier, a local news channel mentioned the shooting at the La Fonda, and the dead man who had checked into the hotel as Jim Singleton, but they weren't sure of his identity. The police were investigating, but I knew the case would remain unsolved forever. The bullets in Pooley's body and in the corridor wall would be untraceable, the weapon had most likely been destroyed, and the man I knew as Hap Blowenfeld was probably far from Santa Fe, probably already on the road to Nevada, where Abe Mann was stopping next. They might have security camera footage of both Hap and me in the lobby of the building, but they will curse their luck that neither of our faces are recognizable, we both seem to be aware of the cameras and are always looking in the opposite direction.

Why had Hap tried to kill me? For the same reason I will put a bullet in both Miguel Cortega and him. Because the end game is the death of nominee Abe Mann at the convention, and we cannot afford to have anyone else fuck up our kill. Whoever hired us wanted three killers to make sure the assignment was done right, was done successfully, but it would be one man ultimately pulling the trigger. It is part of the job, a necessary hazard of the game we choose to play; when multiple killers are hired, multiple killings are assured.

But Hap hadn't killed me; he had killed a part of me, he had killed my only friend in this world, my brother, and for that he would pay with his life, Abe Mann or no Abe Mann.

Darkness. And pain. And Pooley.

After the Levine hit, after I killed the Boston bookie and all of his bodyguards, Vespucci asked for a meeting on the top of a parking garage near the water. The weather had taken a frigid turn, and snow collected on the ground in knee-high drifts, white-washing all of Boston. On the exposed rooftop, the snow piled up unabated, and the wind was implacable as it whipped off the harbour's waters and slammed into us.

Vespucci was alone, bundled up in a thick parka, though he didn't wear a hat. He stood with hard eyes, glaring at me, treating the cold like it was just a nuisance, a fly to be swatted.

'What happened?' he spat at me as soon as I approached him.

'I severed the connection.'

'Severed!' His voice rose over the wind, the contempt unmistakable. 'It was a bloodbath! You killed seven of his men! You left a massacre behind you!'

'I completed my mission.'

'No, Columbus! No! You are mistaken. Your mission was to kill Richard Levine. Only Richard Levine!'

'I did what I had to do to assure the kill.'

He started to say something, then stopped, eyes boring into me. My face was red, but not from the wind stinging it. When he spoke again, his voice was heavy, dolorous.

'Columbus. You are not the right man for this line of work. It hurts me to say this. I believe this to be my fault. I did not . . . how do you say . . . counsel you as properly as I should have. I take responsibility.'

He stamped his feet, but he did not take his eyes off of me. I said nothing, waiting for him to finish what he came here to say.

'Your . . . rampage . . . has caused me some difficulty. The enormity of what you did forced the police

137

to assign an entire task force to the investigation. And not only have the police increased their strength, but a few of the connected families in this city have also put out . . . um . . . what is it . . . feelers . . . to discover who it is that would do this to Levine and his men.'

His eyes softened. I think he saw in my face that I recognized the trouble I had caused him.

'I understand, now, Mr Vespucci. I shouldn't have . . .'

'You shouldn't have continued to see Jacqueline Owens after I told you to stop.'

This caused my face to flush. I wasn't expecting him to bring Jake into this. How did he know?

'Ahh, yes. I know why you did what you did. I know these men discovered your girlfriend. And from there, could have discovered you. I warned you, Columbus. But you would not listen. Pah . . .' He spat on to the ground, like he was spitting my foolishness into the snow. 'So where does that bring us?'

'I'll make it right.'

He shook his head. 'I'm afraid it is too late for that. I wish you the best of luck.'

He started to reach inside his coat, and in an instant, I had a pistol up and pointed at his head. The speed of my draw startled him; I'm not sure what he was expecting, but I was ready. Even in my shame, I was ready.

He looked confused for a moment, then realized where his hand was, and what it must have looked like to me. Slowly, slowly, he pulled from his inside coat pocket a large manila envelope.

'Because of what you did, they will come looking for us. This is the last time we will see each other. I hope you understand.'

With that, he dropped the envelope into the snow and walked away toward the stairwell in the corner of the lot.

The envelope contained enough money for me to dump the apartment and move into an efficiency in Framingham, about thirty miles outside the city. The space was only about five hundred square feet; it had once been a cheap hotel, and the rooms had been converted by putting tiny refrigerators and a sink into the bathrooms. I had to buy a single burner to use as a stovetop, and it was furnished with a Murphy bed, a hard mattress that folded out of the wall.

Pooley moved in four days after I did. I spent a little money on a small car, a Honda, and picked him up at Waxham on the day he was released. He looked the same, gaunt and dishevelled, but somehow healthier. The last couple of years at Waxham had been good to him. He became something of a scrounger, partnered with a few guards, and created a large market for illicit goods inside the Juvey centre. Subsequently, he bought himself a circle of protection from the bigger inmates, and was treated like a boss. He left the place with over five thousand dollars stored in a coffee can buried by a guard outside the walls of the place.

'I think my cell was bigger,' he said when I opened the door to my apartment.

'It probably was.'

'You have any beer?'

'Check the fridge.'

He found a bottle and popped it open, then took a long pull. My only piece of furniture was a lopsided couch I bought at a yard sale. Pooley plopped down on it while I sat on the floor, using one of the walls for a backrest.

'It's good to see you.'

'You look good. You look good.'

We sat for a minute, instantly comfortable, slipping back into our empathy for each other like putting on old jackets. I told him everything, everything I hadn't put into letters, starting with Jake mistaking me for her brother and ending with Vespucci's dismissal of me on the rooftop of the parking garage. He peppered me with questions as I went, asking for details, for clarifications, for specifics. He homed in on Vespucci's role in my life, and fired the inquiries like a machine gun. How much did he charge? How did he get his information? How did he meet his contacts? How many hit men worked for him? Did he do the background research on his own or did he have subordinates? How did he dress? How did he carry himself?

I tried to answer the ones I knew and guessed at the ones I didn't. Pooley was entirely nonjudgmental throughout; in fact, he was fascinated. He asked to see my weapons, and I showed him the pistols, how the racking chamber worked, how to load a clip, how to conceal it on my body.

'I could do it,' he finally said after we had fallen silent for a while, listening to the heavy motor of a snowplough rumbling down the street.

'I don't know, Pooley. Killing a target—'

'No, not the killing part. I don't have the stomach for it. But I could be your fence. Do what Vespucci did.'

My wheels were turning before he finished his sentence. 'How would you go about—?'

'I don't know. Start from scratch, I guess.'

'I'm not sure—'

'I was pretty damned resourceful at Waxham, Columbus.' He let the name out slowly, like his voice was thick with it, a smile on his face. In fact, from that point on, he never called me by my real name. Only the name Vespucci had given to me, my killing name. He continued, 'I'm serious. I am detailed, I blend in, I survive. I negotiated Juvey like a chameleon, all five-foot-nine of me; I was practically running the place before my release. I can get you the details you need to continue doing what you do. I'll pick up where Vespucci left off. I'll be better than him.'

'Where would you even begin to make contacts? It's not a field that invites newcomers. "Hey, you look trustworthy. Wanna kill someone for me?"'

'You let me worry about that.'

'I can't. I'll be worried too.'

'Whatever. Just give me six months. Between what you have and what I have, we don't have to earn another dime for at least a year. If it works, great. If it doesn't, we'll have plenty of time to call it off. Start flipping burgers or packing beer trucks or whatever else it is Waxham graduates do.'

I didn't say anything for a long time. Just pulled on my beer, my back against the wall, tossing it around in my mind. Finally, I looked over at him. He was grinning, his eyes shining.

'You sure you want to go down this road?'

'As sure as you were when you dropped that sewing machine on Cox's fucking head.'

I reached my hand over so we could clink our bottles together. 'Then let's do it.'

Three weeks later, they came for me.


'Three men just stepped out of a Mercedes.'

'What?'

Pooley was sitting on the sofa, his neck craned, shielding his eyes from the sunlight as he peeked out the small window. He just happened to be looking out at exactly the right time.

'They're splitting up, one out front, one heading to the steps, one moving toward the back. Black guys in suits.'

Black guys. Suits. Mercedes. Three things that didn't add up for this dilapidated efficiency in Framingham; three things that might as well have been a warning light on top of a lighthouse tower.

I didn't need any further information. In an instant, I was up and throwing open the case that held my weaponry. Five more seconds and I had two clips popped in place, Glocks double-fisted, racked and ready. Pooley scrambled off the sofa and I tossed him two empty clips. Like lightning, he had a shell-case open and was popping bullets into the clips as though he had been doing it all his life. I would have stopped to smile, appreciate the way his fingers manoeuvered the bullets into place like a piano virtuoso working the keys, but I was all business now.

I crept up to the apartment door, and crouched beside it, then brought one of my guns to the centre of the door, holding it out so the barrel pointed at the wood. Pooley lay down and put his head on the carpet so he could look through the small space separating the bottom of the door from the baseboard. A shadow crossed through the sliver of light in the hallway, and then he spotted two burgundy dress shoes approaching the door.

Pooley didn't hesitate, he nodded his head, giving me the signal to shoot, and I pulled the trigger seven times, blowing holes through the wood, the smell of gunpowder and smoke and blood immediately redolent in my nostrils.

I swung the door open and leaped into the hallway, over the bullet-riddled body of the black man who had come to kill me. He stared vacantly at the ceiling, a look on his face . . . Surprise? Confusion? I didn't stop to puzzle over it, but headed down the corridor for the stairwell that led to the alley behind the building.

A second black man was rushing up the steps just as I reached the landing, and he fired first, catching me in my right shoulder and spinning me backward, knocking me off my feet. He came up to finish me but made the mistake of pausing for a moment over my slumped body. Pooley shot him in the head, at close range, a fountain of red mist spraying the wall and splattering my face like I had showered in blood. He hadn't figured on me having company, hadn't bothered to scout me, to find out if I had any surprises waiting for him. In fact, the amateurish way these shooters had already botched this contract made me think Vespucci might not have sent them. Or if he had been forced to give me up, he maybe held out, did me a favour, gave me one last professional nod. If he had been forced to hire some guys to go after me – if the connected families in Boston had gotten to that olive-skinned Italian – well, at least he sent some minor-league hitters to the plate and gave me a fighting chance.

I kicked in the door on a first floor apartment where I knew the tenant, an electrician, worked on weekdays and wouldn't be home. His apartment had a window facing the front of the building, and Pooley and I squatted next to it to take a look at the third shooter, who was checking his watch, stamping his feet in the cold, and looking impatiently up to my window with increasing concern.

Pooley popped the clip from my Glock, reloaded it, racked it, and placed it in my good hand. Then he cracked the window half an inch, just enough for me to wedge in the barrel of my gun. The third shooter pulled out a piece of paper from the inside pocket of his jacket, checked the address, checked his watch, checked the address again, furrowed his brow, and then . . . wham . . . my first and only shot caught him in the centre of his head, shattering his nose and caving in the front of his face. He stuttered backwards, and then dropped onto the snow-covered asphalt.

Pooley and I quickly gathered my gear, everything we could fit into one large trash bag, and headed into the parking lot for my car. The third shooter still lay dead in the snow, his blood congealed like a halo around his head. The building was tucked into a small street off the main highway, where traffic was non-existent this time of day. Luck was with us, no one had driven into the lot in the five minutes it had taken us to get up to my apartment and gather our possessions.

145

I looked at the dead body, and then noticed the paper still clutched in his hand, the slip he had pulled from his inside jacket pocket.

'Let's go, Columbus. Now, before our luck changes.'

Pooley was right, I should have jumped behind the wheel of the Escort and gotten us out of there, but I wanted to know if that paper had something on it, some clue that would tell me who was trying to kill me and how I could stop it from happening again. I was only being cautious.

I grabbed the paper and sure enough, scrawled in pencil in a barely legible hand was my address here in Framingham, the target's residence, nothing more. At least I thought there was nothing more until I flipped it over.

Scribbled on the other side in that same masculine hand was another address.

Pooley must have seen the colour drain from my face. 'What is it?'

'They have Jake's address.'

I didn't talk. I had the Escort's accelerator mashed to the floorboard, ripping up the highway toward Boston like a missile locked on its target. I was racing blindly, ignoring the increasing amount of pain in my shoulder, my mind focused on one thing, only one thing: getting to Jake. I wouldn't have slowed if God himself had tried to stop me.

'We don't know if they went to her first.'

I didn't answer, and Pooley gave up trying to talk to me. He just sagged back into his chair like the effort was too much.

I blitzed the car into Boston, and flew through intersection after intersection until finally I screeched to a stop outside of her apartment building. I left the car in the street double-parked, not bothering to look for a parking place.

'Columbus! Columbus! Take it easy, for Chrissakes. Do you know how you look? Like a maniac . . .' Pooley was shouting at me but the words weren't registering as I took the steps on her stoop two at a time. I didn't bother to buzz for entry; I just broke the glass door with my fist and twisted the latch from the inside, my hand sticky with blood. I flew up two flights of stairs before reaching her door.

I knocked with my bloody fist; I found I couldn't raise my good hand, the bullet in my shoulder had rendered it useless. Where was she? Oh, God, please tell me they didn't . . . I knocked again, pounded, bam, bam, bam, bam, bam, over and over and over. Please tell me they didn't touch her. Please tell me they didn't. Vespucci told me to stop seeing her and I did, I stopped, I left town without saying good-bye, I didn't phone her, I didn't send her a letter, I was willing to let it die, but not like this, bam, bam, bam, bam, not like this, bam, bam, bam . . .

147

And then the door opened. Jake's face filled the entryway, Jake's beautiful face, my god, she looked fine, healthy, unharmed, untouched, surprised to see me, about to be angry, but then she saw the blood on my shirt, on my hand . . .

'What happened to you?'

She pulled me inside the apartment, her face a picture of concern. I was overwhelmed with relief, couldn't open my mouth.

She spoke instead, 'I've been so worried. For weeks, not a word, not a call. I didn't know what I did to hurt you. I love you so much, I just couldn't understand it.'

She was unbuttoning my shirt, and she gasped when she saw the wound to my shoulder. She didn't think, just immediately darted to the kitchen and snatched up a rag, turned on the faucet and let the water run warm.

I knew then I would have to do the hardest thing I had ever done, harder than killing a man. To end this, to make sure this was finished, to make sure they would never come for her, I couldn't just run away and leave her behind.

She came back, holding the wet cloth, and began to clean my wound, but I grabbed her by the wrist and pushed her back.

'You have to move.'

'What?'

'You have to get out of here. Get your things, whatever you can carry with you in the next five

minutes and get out of here. Go somewhere, anywhere, but get out of Boston and don't come back.'

'What are you talking about?'

'Just do it!'

My voice must have been like a slap to her face,
tears sprung to her eyes.

'I don't understand!'

'I'm a bad man, Jake! I'm worse than bad. I'm a
goddamn nightmare. You don't know a fucking thing
about me.'

'What, what . . .' she sputtered.

'I never fucking loved you. I've been using you as a
fuck rag. Something to sleep with to get my mind off
of all the other shit in my life.'

'What are you talking about?' Her voice was barely
a whisper, a squeak as the tears spilled out and soaked
her mouth.

'You think I give a shit about you? You think I
haven't been fucking twenty other girls just like you?'

'What are you talking about?' she said softer, her
voice breaking.

'Now, I've gone and done it too. There are people
out there who want to hurt you, Jake. People I'm
involved with. I fucking gave them your address and
now they want to see your ass for themselves. See if
you're as ripe as I said you were. '

She took a step back, sobbing . . .

'I can't stop them from coming Jake. And they are
coming. I don't know why I'm even telling you. I

guess I just wanted to give you a sporting chance to get out of here.'

'I don't understand . . .'

'I don't give a shit if you understand or not. You don't leave today, then they come for you.'

'I love you,' she said weakly.

'You gotta leave right now.'

'But I love you!' she screamed, her voice finding a strength that surprised me. 'I don't know what you're talking about, but this isn't you. I don't know who this is, but this isn't you. If you'll tell me what happened, maybe I can—'

And right then I struck her, my bloody fist catching her in the jaw and cracking her cheek, knocking her down to the floor.

'Noooooooo . . .' she started to moan.

I kicked her then, hard, in the stomach. I heard my voice coming out of my throat, disconnected from my body. 'This is everything you need to know Jake. I'm not fucking around. The men I work with, this'll just be the warm-up session. If you're not out of Boston in the next ten minutes, they will be here themselves, do you understand?'

'Whyyyyyyyy . . .' she was whimpering now, the breath knocked out of her.

'Ten minutes. And you forget everything about me. You forget you even knew my name. And if I ever see you again, it'll be the last thing you see. I promise you that.'

I threw the wet rag at her face, spun, and marched out the door, leaving her crumpled frame sobbing on the floor.

Pooley and I watched silently from a nearby alley as Jake limped to her car, threw in a pillowcase filled with possessions, turned it around in the street, and drove away.

I never saw her again.

# Chapter Ten

Violence defines all men. At some point in life's wheel, men are tested. A spanking from dad's belt, a slap across the face, trading blows outside a bar, a broken nose, a bloody mouth, a black eye, a gun pointed in the face, a knife jabbed underneath the ribs. A man's reaction to violence is imprinted upon him like words on a page. He might cower, or shy away, or watch unflinching. He might rise up, or be impassioned, or be aroused. Or he might become violent himself.

And what is the antithesis of violence? Love? Kindness? And can both of these opposites, kindness and violence, Cain and Abel, reside in equal parts in one man? Or does one side battle the other like opposing armies in a long-standing war? And if so, which is the strongest?

I make my way to Nevada, wounded, though not physically, and fatigued. I am no longer on the trail of the man at the top of the page, not yet at least. I am after a different quarry. I am hunting hunters now.

Congressman Abe Mann will not be speaking in Las Vegas, wary of its unseemliness to many voters, conscious of how being photographed in the American Mecca of gambling and money and prostitution will turn off the masses. Rather, he will be making only one stop in Nevada, in the capital, Carson City, before he moves north to Washington state. His press materials will only vaguely mention Nevada, and the dinner in the capital is private and barred from the press.

I do not know Miguel Cortega's modus operandi, but I am confident Hap Blowenfeld will be shadowing the congressman's movements. For that reason, though not that reason alone, Hap will be the first to die.

I drive into Vegas. A man I know lives here; I hesitate to call him a friend. Pooley's job is . . . was . . . to know other middlemen, men looking for contractors to hire for their missions. Often, I meet directly with these merchants, like with Archibald Grant in the warehouse when he handed me the briefcase that changed my life. The middlemen like to eyeball me, see me for themselves, measure me, the way old ladies pick up and shake cantaloupes in the produce section of the grocery. Pooley always said five minutes in a room with me would be enough to shatter any illusions of cheating me, of holding back anything but my promised fee. I hope that is still true.

I drive down Flamingo, heading west toward Summerlin, until I reach a neighbourhood inappropriately named 'Wooded Acres'. Every house is built exactly the same way, a cookie-cutter paradise, a sea of beige stucco and rusty Spanish tile. Each house is adorned with a lawn the size of a postage stamp. The only 'woods' in the neighbourhood are the scrawny palm trees inconsistently spotting the yards.

The nice thing about Vegas suburbs is that discretion is part of the milieu, built into the environment. Everyone seems to walk around with eyes downcast, avoiding direct contact with neighbours. It's like the heat and the barrenness of the landscape have infected the hearts of those who live in the desert. Or maybe too many people are involved in too many impolite occupations.

I park my car at the curb outside of a one-storey house marked by the number 506. I've been here before, twice actually, under different circumstances. But this time is a first for me. This time, I'm looking for help.

The door opens before I knock, and a small Indian man fills the void. He is dark, balding, and has ears too big for his face. Although he is small, he is compact, muscular, like a pit bull. His name is Max, and his voice is raspy.

'Columbus . . .'

155

'Max.'

'Mr Ryan is not expecting you.'

'I need his help.'

This causes Max to pause, blink a few times involuntarily. He waits for more.

'Can I come in?'

'Depends on the kind of help you're looking for, I s'pose.'

'My fence is dead.'

That's all Max needs to hear. He opens the door further and I step inside the foyer. Immediately, two large men frisk me, each with the same dark skin as Max. They could be his sons, or nephews, as they have the same balding pattern on top of their heads. I am directed to a chair next to the door, and I take a seat and wait. The two men stay on my right and left as Max heads away, bare feet shuffling silently over the marble floor. I keep my gaze steady on a spot on the wall five feet away. It is humbling asking a man for help, and I want the right measure of supplication on my face when I greet him.

He makes me wait, a signal he is the person in power in this situation. He wants me to know he recognizes the advantage. But I don't fidget, or cough, or straighten my legs. I just sit in the chair and stare steadily at that spot on the wall. My two bookends want to speak to me, are looking for an opening to chat me up, but I give them nothing. After half an hour, Max returns to the foyer. 'Mr Ryan will see you in his office.'

A large window overlooking an immaculately land-scaped back yard frames the office. A half-clothed woman reclines on a leather sofa pushed up against one wall; I cannot tell if she is awake, asleep, or bored. Ryan sits in a chair, watching a flat-screen television mounted on the wall above the girl. The volume is off, but the screen is alive with graphics showing what the markets are doing all over the world. He is wearing only a swimsuit, though he is not wet.

'How can I help you?' he says without taking his eyes off the screen.

'Pooley is dead.'

'So Max tells me.'

'I'm looking for one thing.'

'Yes?'

'Information.'

'What are you willing to exchange for this one thing?'

'I'll owe you a favour.'

For the first time, Ryan shifts his eyes to me and I feel the full weight of his stare. He measures me, considering. The girl on the sofa stirs, but I don't look, don't drop my eyes; rather I hold Ryan's eyes steadily, like they are connected to mine by a string. He is a man who deals in commodities, and I am dangling a big carrot.

'I take it the information is difficult to come by, considering the payment you're offering.'

'I don't offer it lightly.'

'I understand. What do you need to know?'

'In Carson City, a bag man is going to be looking to dispose of and replace a Beretta 92F nine-millimetre handgun. I need to know the supplier he will approach to make the exchange.'

He tosses these words over in his mind, calculating.

'You got a beef with this bag man?'

'Like I said, Pooley is dead.'

'I see.'

He moves over to the sofa and pats the girl on her exposed hip. Without speaking, she gets up, stretches, and heads out of the room, long legs cutting a swath in front of me until she is gone. He takes her forfeited spot on the couch and sits down heavily, facing me.

'Now I understand. It is not that the information is difficult. It is that the information would be imprudent for me to give.'

'I find that prudence is relative in our line of work.'

This forces a dry laugh from him. 'I agree with you. Here are my terms. Instead of owing me a favour, I wish you to work for me when your current assignment is finished. Permanently. I will be your new fence.'

'With what arrangement?'

'The same you had with Pooley. No more.'

'Why?'

'I've been looking to downsize, and you are what the Russians refer to in this business as a Silver Bear. Have you heard this term?'

I shake my head.

'You've never defaulted on a job. You take a full slate without resting, and you fetch top dollar on the open market. A Silver Bear. I can carry you as my only partner and I'll make more than I've ever made in my life. And I've made quite a bit.'

'You caught me off guard.'

'Well, to use your words, I don't offer it lightly.'

'Then I'll make you this promise. In exchange for the name of this supplier, I will agree to *consider* partnering with you. I don't think you can expect me to give you more than that.'

Ryan smiles broadly. 'It would be imprudent.'

I join him with a smile of my own as respect passes between us like we're exchanging currency.

'And you wouldn't be a Silver Bear if you answered me any other way.'

'You're probably right.'

He stands and folds his arms across his chest.

'Okay, Columbus. I agree to your revised terms. Go to a pay phone on the corner of Desert Inn Road and Paradise. There's a strip mall there with a phone on the north end of it, outside a 7-Eleven. I'll have the name for you by the time you get there.'

Carson City is an uninteresting capital located where Interstates 50 and 395 collide. It is a tiny town, its only purpose to serve its neighbours Reno and Lake Tahoe and the skiers who frequent Squaw Valley and

Diamond Peak and Heavenly. It looks like an afterthought, like a little brother making do with the family's hand-me-down clothes. The buildings are old and pitiful.

I take the Interstate into town and head south, past a mall and a cemetery, until I find the exit for Colorado Street. I'm looking for an industrial park, a concrete slab with no windows, one of those blights on the landscape that looks like it was thrown into place with no more planning than a child scattering his blocks. This one isn't hard to find; the man on the other end of the pay phone in Vegas gave me impeccable directions.

I find a discreet parking lot and roll my beige sedan to a stop. Before I left Vegas, I jettisoned the SUV at McCarran and rented a new car, a Taurus. Through my windshield, I have a view of the only door on the outside of the industrial building, a steel door, solid, with an electronic keypad affixed to the adjacent wall. As an assassin, I have learned about strike moments, about vulnerability, about timing. A fortified target is the most difficult to take down, like Richard Levine holed up in his mansion. A supplier like the one I wish to speak to, like the one I am currently waiting to see, will work out of a bunker, well protected, well guarded, difficult to assault. Which is why I will not attempt to enter the industrial building, the outside of which is just a façade for a fortress. Rather, I'll lie in wait for as long as it takes.

A woman wearing a skullcap and wire-framed glasses emerges from behind the door several hours later. There is only one car in the parking lot, a vintage Mustang painted blue. She climbs inside, pulls the car out of the parking lot, and heads north-west, toward the mountains. She made a mistake choosing a flashy car; it's as easy to follow as if it had a red light on top. I don't know if she is going home, or meeting someone, or stopping at a grocery store, but it doesn't matter; at some point this evening she will be alone, and I will be ready.

It doesn't take long. The woman in the skullcap pulls into a Caribou Coffee parking lot, cuts her engine and steps out of the car to go inside. Her guard is down; my guess is she hasn't been in the supplier business long and has yet to understand the need for caution. When she exits the place holding a paper cup emitting steam, I am lying in wait.

'Tara?'

She jumps, startled, then searches my face, looking for recognition. 'Yes?'

'I need you to come with me.'

A thousand thoughts sweep like storm clouds across her face, all of them dark. I see her eyes dart to the coffee in her right hand, the car keys in her left, and then back to me, sizing me up.

'I suppose you'll be ready if I try to burn you or put these keys in your face?'

'Yes.'

'Is this about some business I did?'

'Do you want to have this conversation in a parking lot?'

She looks at me, processing the question, and then shakes her head. 'What about my car?'

'You should think about driving something less colourful.'

Hap is less than a mile away. He is planning on meeting Tara in thirty minutes to make the exchange, a new gun for old money. He doesn't realize I will be the one meeting him, but that doesn't make him any less of a threat. Assassins are wary by nature, distrustful by training. He might've picked up on something in her voice, a slight rise in inflection letting him know this call was being made under duress, that there was literally a gun to her head. She might have slipped him a code word in the conversation, something agreed upon at an earlier date, a word that is seemingly innocuous, but would signal the true nature of the night's exchange. I think she played it perfectly, innocently, but I'm not Hap on the other end of the line, and I'm not about to approach this confrontation lightly.

I have chosen the cemetery for the exchange, the place I passed on the way to Tara's office. It is after midnight and darker than I expected; the moon is only a fingernail scratching at the night sky. I have been here for hours, adjusting my eyes to the darkness. Not much of an advantage, but sometimes you only need the scales to tip the slightest in your favour to make your kill. I'm not worried about Tara trying to contact Hap and let him know about the trap; she won't be doing much talking for at least a month after what I did to her.

The cemetery is colder at night than I anticipated; the proximity to the mountains brings in a chill wind which seems to permeate right into my skin. The grave markers are small and spread out in neat rows, offering little protection from the breeze. I crouch on the cold earth, my back to a stone marker that reads: MICHAEL MATHESON, 1970–1979, as I watch the front entrance warily, two pistols cocked and loaded, folded into my lap. Hap has lived a few years longer than the boy on whose grave I sit, but I plan on having him join Michael Matheson tonight.

What I don't plan on, what I haven't foreseen, is that Hap is working this job as a tandem sweep. I know from Pooley that three shooters were hired to take out Abe Mann at his party's convention in a little less than a month. What I don't know, not for the next two minutes at least, is that two of them – Miguel Cortega and Hap Blowenfeld – are working this job together.

I am the odd man out, it seems.

# Chapter Eleven

I am bleeding in a cemetery, a fitting place, as though the land itself is beckoning to cover me up like it has so many others. I have two holes in me, one where the bullet entered my side and shattered my rib, and a second where it exited my back. Pools of gore are soaking my shirt and I'll admit I'm a little worried about the blood loss. I am not afraid I will die from this wound, not yet at least, but I am concerned about losing consciousness before I get a chance to take out the second shooter. I'm pretty sure I dropped one of them, at least I think I did. Fuck, I don't know for sure. I am suddenly very tired, like my eyes are filled with sand.

This isn't the first time I've been shot while working a job.

It was my seventh assignment with Pooley. We had settled into a comfortable rhythm; he proved intuitive at setting up a network of contacts and contracts, and resourceful at finding the information I needed to execute my job. He was right. He *was* a natural. He had quickly surpassed Vespucci in every aspect; he had a hunter's eye and a survivor's cleverness – Waxham had given him both – and he was much to credit for our early success.

One client was particularly impressed. I had killed for her recently – a New York job – a Wall Street trader who must've bought when he should've sold. The man had hired a private security firm for protection, but they were sloppy and unprofessional.

Pooley showed up a few weeks after the mark was found in pieces scattered across the George Washington Bridge.

'That job was a big one, Columbus. Our client . . . she's a whale amongst fishes . . . a leading player on the acquiring market.'

'Good . . . I don't want you to have to work so hard.'

He smiled. 'I was thinking I might take a trip. Get out and see the world.'

'You deserve a break.'

'I'm not going on vacation. This is a business trip.'

'Where to?'

'Italy.'

I looked at him skeptically.

'I told you . . . that last client was impressed. She wants to hire you again. Immediately.'

'The mark is overseas?'

'Yeah. I need a month to put the file together. Then you have six weeks to do what you do. She has a specific date she wants you to make the kill. June sixth. In the dead of night.'

'She'll pay for the specificity?'

'It's taken care of.'

I used the four weeks to get my mind right, as Vespucci had taught me. I fell into a routine; there was comfort in rigidity. I worked out hard, running five miles in the mornings, then several hours reading, flipping back and forth between contemporaries and classics: Wolfe and Mailer and Updike and Steinbeck and Maugham and Hemingway. Then a light meal followed by a sparring session at a boxing gym on the south side where everyone paid cash and nobody asked questions. Dinner was at home and I usually watched the news. Then bed. Every day the same. Comfort in rigidity. And I didn't have to think about Jake. I did not want to think about Jake.

Pooley handed me a brown manila envelope, our hellos and how-ya-beens out of the way.

'How was it?'

Pooley shrugged. 'They got a fucked-up way of doin' things over there. They don't like strangers unless they're throwing money around. And even then, they pretty much don't like 'em. But the food was good.'

'You get what you need?'

'It's all there. Our client had some pull.'

'You have any suspicions?'

Pooley shook his head. 'Naah . . . it's no walk in the park because of the specific time she wants it done, but it's nothing you can't handle.'

'I'm going to be in the visitor's dugout.'

'That's true. No home-field advantage.'

'All right, then. Thanks, Pooley. It's good to see you.'

'Good to see you, too, Columbus.'

The name at the top of the page was Gianni Cortino. He was fifty-two years old and currently splitting time between Rome and a coastal town named Positano. He was in the real estate business, but it appeared he had his thumb in a lot of pies: utilities, hotels, restaurants. He was a wealthy man; his net worth was counted in hundreds of millions.

Pooley had done his homework. Like many rich men, Cortino was tight-fisted with his wallet, like he had such a devilish time acquiring the money, it pained him to let any of it escape. His vice was cigars: Cuban Cohibas. He was devoted to his wife, his two sons, and his first grandchild, a boy, Bruno, born just eleven months previous. There had been whiffs of a scandal involving Cortino and a socialist politician in Florence, but the rumours turned out to be planted by an investment rival. As far as Pooley could tell,

168

Cortino was free from graft. No whores, no gambling, no illicit goods, just a successful man in a country that is leery of success.

He also had a bodyguard.

The guard's name was Stephano Gorgio. Gorgio had spent thirteen years in the Italian special forces, mountain division, and had subsequently hired out as a mercenary in the Serbian war in Yugoslavia. His uncle was an early business partner to Cortino, and the two met after Gorgio returned to Italy. He made a proposal to Cortino to come on as his private body-guard, and Cortino fired the security company he had been using and shook hands with Stephano. They had been together seven years.

Gorgio had two bullets in his shoulder, taken when the same investment rival who tried to smear Cortino also tried to kill him. Instead, the rival was choked to death bare-handed by Gorgio, bullets in the shoulder notwithstanding.

In the file were pages and pages of details, attempts at finding patterns in Cortino's life. Did he eat at the same restaurant every day? Did he use the same route to get to work? Did he travel from Rome to Positano at a certain time each month? Use the same roads? Take the same car? The train? There is comfort in rigidity. But there is also death in it.

I arrived in Rome at 3 P.M. and took a taxi to my hotel, a small one in the middle of the city, the Hotel

Mascagni. It was owned by Cortino, one of the first he acquired after he came to Rome with a bit of an inheritance. While he had bought and sold and traded many properties in the twenty years he had been acquiring his fortune, he kept this one throughout. I wasn't sure what clue it would give me about the man, what it would do to help me realize the connection so I could sever the connection, but it was my first tangible piece of the man I came to kill.

The hotel contained only fourteen rooms on six floors and an old two-person elevator built into the tiny lobby. It had a bar and a restaurant – together the size of an American living room – and a small staff who nodded and bowed and gesticulated regularly. The building resonated warmth, the same warmth I got from reading Cortino's file, and I wondered if it was a mistake staying here. I was searching for evil to exploit in the man, and so far I found only charity and kindness.

I took the first two weeks to familiarize myself with the city, not as a tourist would, but as a rich businessman might. I avoided the ancients: the coliseum, the pantheon, the Vatican, instead concentrating on the busy commercial streets named after months: Settembre, Novembre. I ate at restaurants I knew Cortino haunted, places specializing in seafood and pasta, but managed to avoid seeing him until I set my foundation, until I began to think like a local, establish my roots.

The third week I took a train from Rome to Naples and then hired a car to take me from Naples to Positano. I travelled the way Cortino did – although it was rare and inconvenient for such a wealthy man to travel by rail and car between the cities, Cortino lived as he did when he had no money. I imagine it was a way for him to remind himself of the struggle, that if he lost touch with his rise, he'd give way to his fall. It was a trait I admired.

The train was clean and comfortable and not at all unpleasant, a mixture of tourists and natives on their way to the coast. The station in Naples was the opposite, a dirty latrine in a bathroom town. Dark-faced con men looked for gullible tourists, but they only glanced my way before homing in on easier prey.

A driver took me to Positano in a white Mercedes van, following the winding, narrow road down the coastline. His English was limited and I was glad; I didn't feel like chatting. I knew Cortino lived high up on the hill overlooking the city, and with a population of less than 4,000, he would be a well-known figure in the town. I had read in the file that Positano was built into the side of a hill feeding down to the sea, but I wasn't prepared for the reality. Positano is a vertical city; the buildings seem to sit one on top of another as they move straight up a steep gradient, like a grocer's shelf that allows you to see the front of everything you're buying. Red and pink and yellow and white and peach and tan, the buildings cut into the green foliage like they are part of the mountain, only stopping when they reach the sky or the sea.

Tourists were everywhere. Fat Germans with fanny packs jostled each other as they cruised from shop to shop while Vespas plunged down the streets like a swarm of gnats, everyone and everything heading in one direction . . . down to the ocean. I loved the place. I loved the order of it and the simplicity of it and the singular logic of it; the church bells and the black sand and the quaint shops and the narrow alleys and the coffee makers and the gelato makers and the pasta makers and I was pleased I would kill Cortino here. Not in the bustle of Rome, where it would be infinitely easier to get away, not on the train or the station in Naples where the grime and the desperation were palpable. No, I was glad to be a part of this place, to create a new legend for a town that looked old and felt older. I don't know why I was happy, except to say for the first time, I had a strong feeling about a *place*, maybe my place in it. Like the job I did, the killing I did, the life I led up to this point were somehow reflected in this town, cut impossibly against the gradient, always on the precipice, always just a heavy rain from tumbling into the sea. There was something artistic about it, and infinitely sad. There was a warmth to it, not just a physical warmth but a psychological one, and if I couldn't have Jake, if I couldn't have someone who could cover me like a blanket, then maybe I could find security and understanding and promise and depth in this place, this impossible town.

I checked into a hotel positioned about halfway up the hill. My suite offered a deck overlooking the cliff and the sea and if I sat in the darkness inside my room, all I needed to do was lift my eyes to the top of the window to see Cortino's house, a salmon-coloured mansion with high arched windows at the hill's summit. According to Pooley's file, he would be coming to town one week before I was to kill him.

I took the time to adjust to the place and have it adjust to me. I was just another *turista* in a town that fed itself on *turistas,* and I bled into the scene gradually, the way watercolours fade the longer the brush is applied to the canvas. I bought a straw fedora and wore it poorly; I lunched in the open-air cafés perched above the ocean; I milled through the souvenir shops and pressed my face to the glass of the pastry counters. I took a boat to Capri – Newbury Street covering an island – and came back with a sunburn. I blended in, but never forgot why I was there.

'Would you like coffee, cappuccino, Coke?'

The waitress looked affable; she had pale blue eyes and tanned cheeks.

'Coffee . . . *grazi.*'

'*Prego.* Where are you from?'

'Los Angeles. United States.'

'It is my dream to go there. Very beautiful.'

'It is the dream of Americans to come here.'

'Ahh . . .' She looked down at the sea, a sight that had lost its magic for her long ago. 'I'll bring your coffee.'

I waited for her to return and greeted her with a smile. The place wasn't full. 'How many people live in Positano?'

'Four thousand, more or less.'

'Everyone knows each other?'

'Oh, yes.'

'Any Americans?'

'Yes . . . summer houses. An English couple too.'

'How much does a house cost here?'

'Depends on how high up you are . . . or how close to the beach.'

I sipped my coffee. She didn't look in a hurry to go anywhere else, so I pressed on. 'Like, say, that one up there.'

'The Cortinos. Wealthy family.'

'The house looks big.'

'It is. Five . . . how do you say . . . rooms for sleeping . . .'

'Bedrooms?'

'Yes.' She smiled. 'My guess is . . . two million euros . . .'

I let out a low whistle.

'Yes, expensive. But they are nice family. They helped rebuild the church. Mrs Cortino . . . her legs . . . how is it . . . don't work. It is . . . much pity.'

'She uses a wheelchair?'

'Yes.'

'Must be difficult in this town.'

'Yes . . . but he takes care of her. Makes sure she still goes around.'

'That's very nice.'

'Yes.'

A couple of noisy Austrian tourists came in. She smiled, rolled her eyes, and went to help them find a table. I sipped my coffee, thinking.

His wife, crippled. In this town, it must be extremely difficult; the place wasn't exactly built wheelchair-friendly. None of this was in the file. Why did Pooley censor it? Did he think it would affect me? Was he concerned that after I had used my time to measure this man, I would find he was a good man, a man with no capacity for evil, with nothing to exploit?

I first saw Cortino and his bodyguard Gorgio a week later. He visited a church near my hotel, a stone edifice painted the same colour as the cliff so it blended into the rock. The exterior was bleak, lacking the ornate iconography of most Catholic churches. I knew it was one of the first things he'd do when he returned to Positano; his file noted that he always walked to the church, lit two candles, and kneeled before the altar. For whom he lit the candles, I didn't know, maybe one for each of his deceased parents.

I sat at a nearby Mediterranean restaurant, eating prawns silently, careful not to attract attention. Cortino looked grave as he moved inside the church. Twenty minutes passed as I ate my seafood, waiting for him to emerge. When he exited, his face was transformed, beatific. This surprised me. Could a man's attitude really be improved so radically from the simple act of kneeling? What had he found in there? What words had his lips whispered? I discovered I was staring at his peaceful face, fascinated, and when my gaze flicked to the bodyguard, Stefano Gorgio, the man was eyeing me.

What a goddamn mistake. I looked past the bodyguard, through him, like I was just another daft tourist enjoying a taste of local scenery. This must've satisfied him, because Gorgio shuffled after his boss, helping him into a parked Mercedes two-seater. I didn't lift my eyes again; I just picked at my shrimp until I heard the car disappear around the corner, heading down the hill. Fuck. Gorgio was good, a real professional, he would certainly remember seeing me if I popped up near his boss's home.

I went back to my hotel room and turned off the lights, pissed . . . pissed at myself, pissed at the missing information from the file, pissed that everything I learned about Cortino made me . . . what? Envious? Of him? Of this life?

It hit me like a grease fire. Is that what I would exploit? My own jealousy? Not evil in him but evil in me? It spread out before me like a Polaroid coming into focus. How does an assassin bring down a good man? He summons up his own iniquity; he measures himself against the man and feeds on the distance he falls short. And where would that road lead, when there was no connection to sever? What price would I pay for focusing my hate on myself?

I holed up in the hotel and the few restaurants on my side of the hill until June 6 arrived, the day I was supposed to put a bullet in Gianni Cortino. That morning, I rented a scooter from a tourist trap near the main town centre, entering when the place was most crowded. I was just one more American tourist in a sea of Anglo faces.

I headed down the single town road and then up the hill, black helmet obscuring my face. I wanted to take a peek at Cortino's house from the street, so I slowly motored by, using my peripheral vision to take measure of the place. Fortunately, there was no room for anything remotely resembling a yard. The house's roof was level with the street, stone steps led down from the street to the front door. There was no gate, no security cameras. Positano was too quiet and peaceful and small and remote to worry about crime, an illusion I would shatter by sunrise tomorrow. From Pooley's file I knew a side door was accessible from below; my partner believed the side door was most likely Stefano Gorgio's private room. I motored on, just one of a thousand scooters passing by that day.

★　　★　　★

At two in the morning, I checked out of the hotel, carrying only a small backpack. I explained that I had a car waiting for me at the bottom of the hill and the night clerk had me sign the requisite papers before settling back down to read the French newspaper *Le Monde*. Since I had dressed all in black the last few days, he didn't notice anything unusual about the way I wore it now. I set out on foot, my pace quick. While Positano has a lot of things, it doesn't have an active nightlife. The street was deserted, the only sound an occasional dog barking.

It took me an hour to descend the hill and then climb the road leading to Cortino's house. One car rolled up behind me, but I pressed into the nearby foliage and it passed without slowing. When I reached the bend that included Cortino's house, I ducked to his side of the street and disappeared over the hedge separating his house from the road. Instead of using the stone steps to head to the front door, I slid along the vines to approach the side door from above, a manoeuver that kept me from having to cross the bay windows lining the oceanside of the house.

The side door was cracked open. Not wide, but cracked enough for me to see the gap. Why? Was this the way Gorgio aerated his room, letting in the ocean breezes? I didn't think it likely, not for a bodyguard. Warning bells rang in my ears.

I moved to the door, listening carefully for a full minute, but I didn't hear a sound inside, no snoring, no breathing, nothing. I armed myself and discarded the backpack in the brush, held my breath, and pushed the door open a crack. The hinges didn't make a sound, thank God for that. No response. I ducked my head in and out of the room in a split second, just enough time for me to scan the room or draw fire. My eyes had long since adjusted to the darkness outside, so the dark room held no secrets.

The room was empty; a single queen-sized bed sat in its centre, undisturbed. I crept in quietly, barely breathing, my senses alert like a trapped animal, listening for anything. The hairs on my arms stood up as though maybe they could pick up on vibrations in the air and shoot me a warning. Why was that door open? Why on *this* night? For the first time, I realized how nonchalantly I had approached this job. I had found nothing to hate about my target, nothing to exploit, and so had granted him a free pass, had woefully underestimated the difficulty of killing this man, had failed before I began. I vowed not to make that mistake again.

Cortino's bedroom was on the same side of the house. I made my way out of the room, gun leading the way. I didn't hate him before, but I hated him now. Hated him for giving me nothing to hate. A few more feet down the hallway, and I was standing outside the master bedroom. There was something in the air now, something pungent, but I couldn't place the smell.

I tested the door and found it unlatched. I pushed into the room, slowly, carefully, soundlessly.

The odour of blood hit me flush in the face. There were two dead bodies in the bed, Cortino and his crippled wife propped up against the headrest, staring back at me with hollow eyes. Against the far wall slumped a third dead body, Stefano Gorgio; most of his face simply wasn't there.

I had come to kill a man who was already dead.

It took me a second to process this when I heard a noise behind me. I spun to see a woman standing in the hallway, smiling, a gun drawn.

Fuck. She had a date she wanted the job done. June sixth. In the dead of night. She even paid for the specificity. And now she had the perfect fall guy delivered to her doorstep, a stranger holding a gun, another corpse she could leave behind. The police would have a field day.

'Pooley told me you were good,' she said. 'And right on time.'

With that, she shot me in the chest.

# Chapter Twelve

Twenty minutes have passed and I realize I am alone in the cemetery in Carson City, Nevada. Whether Hap Blowenfeld or Miguel Cortega are wounded or whether they think they'd have trouble taking me, they failed to finish the job. They will regret this decision.

I struggle to my knees and the pain in my side is almost unbearable. Using the dead boy's headstone for support, I work myself to my feet and peer around. Empty. The sky is lightening in the east; clouds like pink fingers hang low on the horizon. I need to get out of here.

I hobble toward the gate where I left my car, hoping, willing it to still be there. The sun rises above the horizon and a tombstone to my left catches my attention. It is speckled with red droplets; they catch the sun like gemstones set into a ring. I crane my neck around the marker, not wanting to lose any time but I have to look goddammit, I have to see what made blood splatter like paint across the marble tombstone. First I see a hand, immobile, on the ground, and then a torso, and finally an unfamiliar face, still breathing.

I move closer, cautiously, until I see clearly he has dropped his pistol and is clutching a wound in his abdomen, a gut shot, the worst way to go. Somehow, he has made it through the night and is still alive.

'Miguel Cortega?'

His eyes shift to meet mine, but he makes no effort to talk. His breathing is raspy, like air whistling through a pinched pipe. Now I see he's been hit twice, a slug in the stomach and one through his lung.

'You were working this job with Hap. Together.'

He doesn't reply.

'Where's he going next? Where's he supposed to make the kill?'

Cortega just stares at me, blankly, his pupils dilating. A little pink stream curls from the side of his mouth and spills out into two tendrils down his cheek.

He's got another hour to live, maybe more. I could put a bullet in him to put him out of his misery, but I don't feel merciful. Fuck him and fuck Hap.

I hobble away, the pain like a hot iron pressed to my side, and am fortunate to find my car, untouched, in the parking lot.

Thankfully, roadside gas stations have evolved into full-fledged grocery stores, and I find enough bandages and anti-bacterial cream to clean my wound until I can get to a proper pharmacy. The clerk gives me the requisite once-over, but the blue ink of his jailhouse tattoos tells me he isn't going to ask any questions or raise any eyebrows. I drive on until I find a Motel Six. I check the wound, dress it as properly as I can, turn off the light, collapse on the bed, and sleep for eighteen hours.

The road between Lake Tahoe and Seattle is dry and barren. The eastern side of Washington is a desert, and the miles roll by plain and indistinguishable. I can only make it about two hundred miles before my side throbs so badly it threatens my consciousness, but I don't mind falling behind schedule. The convention is still over a week away, and Abe Mann is planning to dawdle in Seattle and Portland to rest up for the big event. He isn't scheduled to show up until the penultimate evening when he 'sneaks' on stage to give a kiss to his wife after her keynote speech. This is supposed to be a surprise but is as pre-planned, practised, and scripted as a Broadway show. He isn't supposed to return to the stage until the final night, when he makes the most important speech of his political career. What *is* unscripted, what will be a real surprise, is he won't be returning to the stage at all.

I check into an Economy Inn in Walla Walla, Washington. It is on a strip with four other hotels just like it, way-stations for the tired and dispossessed.

On the television, Mann stands with the Port of Seattle spread out behind him, thousands of containers stacked like a multicoloured maze serving as his backdrop. He's talking about the need for tighter port security and stronger counter-terrorism measures and tougher restrictions on containers and more dollars invested to secure our borders. His preacher hand gesture punctuates every phrase, and his face looks properly stern, his eyes fierce and determined. He has found a topic he believes in, and it shows in his eyes. For a moment, I wonder what those eyes will look like when I kill him at close range. I wonder if I'll get him alone, so I can tell him his killer is also his son. I wonder if he'll even care.

A pharmacy sits on top of a hill on the opposite side of town. Without Pooley, without a middleman, I have no way to see a doctor or procure a prescription. As it is, I have to heal myself with over-the-counter medication, but I have done this long enough to know what to look for, how to up the dosages, how to dress my wound to stave off infection. I fill a basket with tubes of campho-phenique, rolls of gauze, bottles of extra-strength Tylenol gel-caps, boxes of Q-tips and spools of medical tape. I am fighting a fever now, and if the clerk looks at me strangely, I don't take notice. I pay in cash and leave quickly.

A tiny church shares the parking lot with the pharmacy. I didn't notice it on the way in, but as I toss the bags into the car, light reflects off the stained glass and catches my eye. My mind seizes on that look on Cortino's face as he came out of the church built into the hill in Positano. The look of peace he had somehow found inside that building and carried out with him. Improbably, I find my feet moving toward the church door.

The sanctuary is empty. No more than twenty pews divide into two columns and point toward a small riser holding a pulpit. A simple mahogany cross decorates the back wall. The afternoon light filters through the stained glass outside and bathes the room in soft ethereal light. I think about Pooley and suddenly my legs feel tired. I sit down and steady my breathing until a feeling of nausea passes. How long I rest, I can't be sure.

'Afternoon.'

A young man stands in the aisle, awash in the light from the windows. He is dressed conservatively, with a blue shirt tucked into grey slacks.

'Afternoon,' I manage.

'Are you okay?'

'Just resting.'

'You came to the right place.'

I am hoping if I stay very still he will go away. Instead, he sits in the pew in front of me and swivels his head to face my direction.

'Are you new to the church?'

'Just passing through.'

'A traveller?'

'Yes, sir. I'm sorry to slip in here . . .'

He waves his hand. 'A church with locked doors is like screen doors on a submarine. Purposeless. My name is Dr Garrett.' He extends his hand and I shake it. For the life of me, I can't figure out why I haven't headed for daylight. Fuck, am I tired.

'You look young for a preacher.'

'That's kind of you to say. But I've been doing this for a long time. Twenty-somethin' years now.'

I smile weakly.

'Tell you what. I'll let you speak to the Lord all you want. If you need me, my office is just on the other side of that door.'

He stands up, and I'm not sure what I'm doing, but I hear myself say, 'Preacher?'

'Yes?'

He pauses standing over me.

'Aren't you worried about danger coming through the door?' I hear myself saying. But the voice isn't mine, not exactly. At least it doesn't sound like me.

The preacher looks at me thoughtfully. 'No. This place is about comfort, about sanctuary . . .'

But he stops suddenly as I stand up and grab him by the throat. His eyes change quickly, from confidence to surprise to terror. Well, that's not right. It's not I watching those eyes, not I pulling the pistol out of the small of my back, not I whose right hand explodes in a blur and smashes the pistol into the side of his face, smashes him again, pistol-whipping

186

him furiously, bam, bam, bam, over and over and over . . .

'Why?' the preacher manages as he goes down between the pews.

And I don't know how to answer the question, I don't know why, I don't know who this person is beating a defenseless face on a defenseless preacher in a defenseless sanctuary until that face is a mask of blood and gore.

'Fuck, fuck, fuck,' the person who is not I mutters, and then spits on the moaning lump on the floor.

In five minutes, I am on the road again, heading west through the desert, the infinite white line of the highway sliding underneath my tires. It is not I who holds the wheel steadily, the pain in my side forgotten. It is not I with a grin on my face.

Clouds hang like a ceiling over downtown Seattle, low and grey and threatening. To the south, Mt Rainier fills the horizon like a wart on the landscape. Something about it seems foreign here, wrong, like it broke away from a mountain chain and moved off to sulk on its own. This morning it is blindfolded, its peak lost above the clouds.

It is time to focus. I have yet to set up even the basics for my kill and subsequent escape. Since Positano, since I managed to crawl to the road with two bullets in me, since I somehow stole a Vespa and somehow fought off losing consciousness and somehow negotiated sixty miles to Naples in the dead of night without being stopped by the police and somehow holed up until Pooley could get to me, get a doctor to me, since that evening when I walked into a room to make a kill but instead walked into a trap where I was going to be the fall guy, since then I have put much greater thought into my assassinations. Vespucci placed importance on the psychology of the killing business, but in retrospect he paid short shrift to executing the executions. His job was to pull together a wealth of information, giving his assassins the best avenues to kill a target. But he left the actual task to his hired killers, left the method and the deed and the strategy to his men.

I had planned to get to Abe Mann at a speech he was to give in Los Angeles the day before the convention started. The only rule I had was that the kill had to be the week of the convention, but the exact time and place were left to my discretion. I knew he had plans to speak using a hundred local firefighters behind him, and I was angling Pooley to get the contact information about who arranged the 'staging' of these events. Once the information was obtained, I would manipulate either the person or the list or one of the firefighters so I would be included in the event, so there would be a spot for me on the dais behind him. I knew ten different fire stations would have to send men to fill those spots and there would be little overlap in the ranks. An unfamiliar face wouldn't be noticed, especially if I had set the table, so to speak, had the proper credentials and ID and documentation to pass myself off. I would use a Secret Serviceman's gun.

But that plan shattered like a broken mirror when Hap killed Pooley in Santa Fe.

Hap. Of course. Hap brought himself into the equation and Hap became the solution. By taking away my options, Hap *became* the option. I would find Hap Blowenfeld, I would locate him and instead of killing him, I would piggyback on his plan to kill the congressman. If I got lucky, I would leave him for dead, framed in the process, like the woman in Positano tried to do to me.

# Chapter Thirteen

I am fortunate the bullet passed through my side without shattering a rib or puncturing an organ. I'm fortunate it is a clean wound and the bandages and medication have stanched the bleeding and diminished the pain. I feel better. Not whole, not onehundred percent, but better.

Now to find Hap. The supplier route to Hap failed spectacularly; that door was obviously shut, and I would have to open a new door. This time I didn't want to kill him, just find him and follow him.

I get up, shower, redress my bandages, dress casually – black jeans and black T-shirt – and take Interstate 5 into downtown.

I exit at Madison and head to the waterfront. I want to see the Pacific, to stare out at the horizon where the dark water meets the light sky. I find a metered parking space and make my way across a small patch of grass where businessmen and women lie in the sun, content to feel intermittent sunlight, if only for a few fleeting seconds.

I stand at the water's edge for an hour. Dark water meeting light sky. It is time to finish this. To forget connecting with Abe Mann. I realize I no longer need to connect with him, we were connected long before I saw his name at the top of the page. I only need to sever the connection, once and for all.

It hits me there, watching the light and the darkness disappear into each other. The connection I need to sever isn't the one between Mann and me. The connection I need to sever is the one holding me back.

I find a pay phone and dial a number from memory. After a brief exchange with Max, he puts me through to Mr Ryan in Las Vegas.

'I agree to your offer.'

'You will let me represent you? Exclusively?'

'You have your Silver Bear.'

I hear an exhale through the line, like he is allowing himself a moment for this to sink in. It is a rare moment of emotion for a stoical man, and it pleases me.

'I am very happy. You will not regret this.'

'I'm sure I won't and I am happy as well, Mr Ryan.'

'Call me William. We are partners.'

'William.'

'You are finishing a job now?'

'Yes. It will be finished by the end of the week.'

'And after, how soon would you like to work again?'

'Give me two months.'

'Where would you like to work?'

'The Northeast, preferably.'

'Is that your home?'

'Yes, Boston.'

'Ahhh. There is a lot of work in New York right now.'

'That would be fine.'

'I'll have a file for you in two months.'

'Great.'

He waits, knowing I have more to tell him.

'There is one other thing, William. One thing I need immediately on my current job. I don't have Pooley any more, and I will give you his commission for this assignment.'

'Yes, that will be fine. What can I get you?'

'I need you to arrange a meeting.'

'Yes?'

'There is an East Coast fence named Vespucci. I worked for him originally. He brought me in. We had a bit of bad blood when we went our separate ways.'

'Yes?'

'I need a meeting . . .'

'Okay . . .'

'In Seattle.'

'I believe this will be difficult.'

'That's why I'm joining you. Exclusively. Because your reputation is you handle difficulty very well.'

'Yes, I see. When?'

'As soon as possible.'

'Yes. How may I reach you?'

'I'll call you in twelve hours.'

'Yes. It will be done.'

I walk to the Pike Place Market, a short quarter-mile from the sea. As far as tourist traps go, this isn't a bad one, and I find it sparsely crowded at this time of day in the middle of the week. I buy a newspaper and eat some grilled salmon and stare at nothing and think of nothing. The fish tastes bland. Outside, it starts to rain.

The meeting is set for a bar at the Sea-Tac airport. This is a smart choice by Vespucci for obvious reasons. Shooters like to meet in airport terminals; security being what it is, it is damn near impossible to sneak in a weapon. I have yet to hear of a man killed in an airport bar; the locale is a safe-haven for dangerous men to meet and exchange pleasantries. And information.

I purchase a ticket to Toronto I don't intend to use and arrive an hour early to get my bearings. The bar is named C.J. Borg's, a small place with a single entrance and exit, dimly lit and half full, just off the Alaskan Airways terminal. I pick a booth in the back where I can watch the entrance. Even in a high security zone, I don't want to take any chances.

Vespucci is unmistakable as he waddles into the bar, squints as his eyes adjust to the absence of light, and then finds me in the corner. He hasn't changed, his hair is still dark, and his weight looks the same. The only difference is his eyes; there is a weariness there I didn't notice before, like whatever pleasure he once got out of life has long since evaporated.

'Hello, Columbus.'

'Hello.'

He keeps his expression, and his voice, even.

'You have been well?'

'No. Not very well, Mr Vespucci.'

'Yes. I know as much. I am sorry about your fence.'

'Sorry doesn't quite cover it.'

'No. I understand.'

'Here's what I want. I want you to serve up Hap Blowenfeld or whatever his real name is. I know we got tripled up on this job and I know no one asked for it and I know we're spending more time trying to kill each other than trying to eliminate the target. I've already disposed of Miguel Cortega. I will do the same to Hap.'

'Why should I . . . how is it you say . . . serve up my own man?'

'Because I'm going to get to him one way or another. And I'm going to finish this job.' I level my eyes at him. 'And if you don't help me, I'm going to finish you.'

He starts to say something but I interrupt . . .

'Jurgenson in Amsterdam. Sharpe in D.C. Korrigan in Montreal. Reeves in Chicago. Cole in Atlanta. You know of these?'

He nods his head.

'I put them all down. They were supposed to be impossible and I got to them all. I've never targeted anyone off-job, but if you don't help me, you will be my first.'

He leans back, contemplating.

'You've changed,' he says at last.

'You changed me.'

His whole body sags a little in the chair, like I made the weight on top of his shoulders heavier. He leans forward, then pauses, like he wants to pick his words carefully.

'I know where she lives.'

For a moment, I say nothing. There is no need for him to explain whom *she* refers to; I know who she is without giving the name. It is a calculated move on his part, and if he is expecting me to blink, he played the wrong cards.

'I don't care.'

'Ahhh . . . I think you do care, Columbus. I think you would very much like to know what I know.'

'You don't think I could've gotten to her a thousand ways since that job eight years ago? I'm the one who sent her packing. Don't forget that.'

'You sent her packing because you care for her. You kicked her in the stomach because you care for her. You haven't tracked her down because you care for her. Maybe you haven't changed as much as I thought.'

I start to say something but it is his turn to interrupt.

'You threaten my life, Columbus, but I can say to you truly, I don't give a steaming pile of shit for my life. It is ending soon, and I am at peace. Whatever punishment I have coming, it will not be in this life, I can assure you. Whatever ways you can make me hurt, it will be a blessing. I have much . . . I have many regrets, I mean to say.'

His eyes are rheumy and his lids are heavy, but I am sure this is no ploy; he is searching for truth in a life filled with death and what he sees in the abyss makes him blink. He hasn't finished what he wants to tell me.

'You think pulling the trigger is difficult? You think executing the job is difficult? Think of what I do, what your fence did for you. We research these targets, these men, these women, we find out every intimate detail of their lives so another may end that life. We make the blueprints of their death. We take away their free will. We know the future. We know as we study them in the present, they have little time to live. We know it, but *they* don't know it, do you understand? It is a rare power, reserved for God.'

He moves his coffee cup from one side of the table to the other. 'Pah. Forgive me. I am old and tired. I

197

cannot explain what this means. My words do not represent me well.'

I stare at him as though for the first time. This old man who brought me into this life and now lives with regret. I had not thought of the toll it takes on the fence, the middleman, to compile those files I savour. I am able to make the connection and sever the connection, but he – and Pooley – only connected and then watched someone else do the severing. The fee exacted on them was both psychological and physical; I could see it now in Vespucci's bloodshot eyes.

I discover here, in this moment, I will fail. I let this assignment get the best of me, take the best *from* me. I let my rejected past overtake me and I ignored all the warning signs because of my own hubris. My threat to Vespucci has been rendered empty, and he knows it. Not because he manipulated me, but because he disarmed me by simply telling the truth.

I realize we haven't said a word to each other for several minutes. He is looking at me the way a scolded schoolchild looks at a teacher, waiting for me to dole out punishment, waiting for a blow that will never come.

Finally, I stand up, lost.

'Are we finished?'

'Yes.'

He lets out a breath and stands. 'Well. It was good seeing you Columbus. I mean that.'

I don't answer, and he shuffles away. It is dark outside when I leave the terminal. The rain is relentless.

I return to my hotel like a man walking in his sleep. I have no plan B, no backup, no contingency for getting to Abe Mann. I have every confidence I can get a bullet into him, but I have no way to escape, and I do not make suicide runs. I have nowhere to turn. I am out of ideas.

I will have to go south, to Los Angeles, and observe, and hope Hap doesn't sniff me out first, and look for an opening. If I have a chance for a clean shot, I'll have to take it and rely on my instincts to keep me alive and out of jail. I have no other options.

I begin packing my few things, when there is a knock on the door. I snatch up a pistol, crouch low next to the doorframe, and say, 'Yeah?'

Vespucci's voice comes through softly from the other side of the wall. 'Columbus. It is me. I am . . . unarmed.'

Something in his voice sounds dead and hollow, like he is damned, soulless. I lower my gun, stand up and open the door without hesitation. He must have followed me here from the airport, but the tone in his voice is not dangerous.

He is holding an envelope; his eyes appear lifeless, just dark circles in a dark face.

'I will not give you Hap.'

I don't say a word. He didn't come here to tell me what I already knew. He extends his hand and I take the proffered envelope.

'Candidate Abe Mann will be alone in this hotel room exactly twenty-four hours before he is to address the convention. Do not ask me how I know this or why I know this. It is information Hap has, and now it is information you have. The playing field is levelled, as they say.'

I am unsure how to respond, so I just nod.

'I do not do this for you because I owe it to you. I do it for me. Do you understand?'

'Yes.'

It is his turn to nod. He studies my face, like he is trying to commit it to memory, like this will be the last time he looks upon it.

'It is too late for me.' And with that, he moves away, into the shadows and darkness and implacable rain.

# Chapter Fourteen

I stand in a field on the outskirts of Portland, Oregon, with a thousand citizens, watching Abe Mann talk on a raised platform. He is angry and it seems, for the first time since I've been stalking him, speaking off the cuff, without notes, without a script.

'. . . Politics in this country have descended into a two-party demigod where lines are drawn on every issue before anyone can manage a true original thought. It is a system built on discord. A system fostering sticks instead of carrots. We talk about extending olive branches and meeting in the middle and working with the other side of the aisle but it's all . . . well . . . horse-pucky.'

The crowd applauds nervously, like it senses something here is a little out of whack.

Mann continues like he didn't hear the clapping. 'I mean, come on, people. It's like two dogs tied to the same chain pulling in opposite directions. They can't get anywhere; they just stay in the same place, grunting and growling, impotent. Well, I tell you right now, someone needs to point those dogs in the same direction or put 'em both out of their misery.'

I am watching Mann's handlers on the side of the dais as they stew uncomfortably, trying and failing to get their candidate's attention. I notice him look their way, then his eyes go right back to the audience, ignoring their signals to cut it short. A fat guy standing to the side in an ill-fitting suit looks like he's about to go apoplectic, but Mann just keeps on talking.

'Here's the problem with that big capitol building on the hill. When the going gets tough, the weak ones cave. "The best lack all conviction while the worst are full of passionate intensity." No one finishes anything. Not how they meant to finish, I mean.'

His eyes scan the crowd, fall right on me like he's singling me out, and then pass on.

'They start out with the best intentions but there you go, two parties digging at each other every chance they get and with the pork, and the gravy on the pork, and the salt on the gravy on the pork, by the time you've been kicked in the teeth a couple hundred times, what you started out doing doesn't look a cock and bull close to what it ended up being. No one finishes anything. The centre cannot hold. No one wants to . . .'

His microphone cuts out on him. It takes him a few sentences to realize what has happened, that he's been emasculated. He looks over at his handlers hotly, but then defeat spreads across his face like a virus. I am reminded of that skittish dog outside of McDonalds in Santa Fe trying to get to his feet, trying to force his legs to work again, trying to somehow shake off the brute force that had crippled him, and failing over and over and over.

Mann's own men have choked him, put the muzzle on him, and he shrugs and walks off the stage, his eyes cast down. He has been silenced, but his words still hang over the crowd, hang over me, until all of us shuffle away silently, like we're leaving a funeral.

I did walk off a job once without killing the target, without completing the mission. Just a year ago, last winter. I didn't want to work, had decided to take a break and recharge my batteries, but Pooley fielded an offer double our usual fee and I figured I could rest later, when the weather grew warmer.

I was suspicious about the fee, double wages could only mean this particular job would be unusually difficult. I had been wary since Positano, and I refused to make the same mistake twice.

The target's name was Jaquelle Val Saint, a French woman living in Dallas, Texas, a mistress according to the file Pooley cobbled together. She had changed her name to Monique Val Saint, though Pooley wasn't sure why or what the significance was. He made notes in the file indicating the fence he was dealing with on the other side of the table had been extremely reticent about giving information. Nevertheless, Pooley had done his job well, painstakingly accounting for all the details in Monique's life.

Her lover was Jacob J. Adams, a major real estate player in North Dallas. He had built a small fortune buying up factories, remodelling them, and then leasing the warehouses to manufacturers all over the Southwest. In the course of growing his business, he had greased enough connected palms to kindle small-time political aspirations of his own. It didn't take a lot of deduction to imagine how Monique ended up with a price on her head.

From the file Pooley put together, I knew Monique lived in a loft apartment with a view of downtown Dallas out her living room window and a swimming pool on the roof so she could keep her skin tanned golden brown. I saw she exercised five times a week at a local health club, but that number had dwindled to only once in Pooley's last week of surveillance. She had put on a little weight; maybe that had added to Mr Adams's dissatisfaction.

According to the file, Adams's wife was unaware of the ongoing affair. Pooley was confident of it. This was important information; if the wife had plans of her own to confront Ms Val Saint, it could cause me logistical problems. A heated exchange could conceivably complicate things at the wrong time, either bringing unwarranted outsiders – curious neighbours, or, worse, the police – into the equation, which would make my job all the more difficult. I wanted to move fast on this one: get in, get the job done, and get out.

I flew to Dallas, rented a car, and drove to an area called Deep Ellum. A brick factory had been converted to giant lofts on Canon Street, and I'm sure Adams had negotiated a good deal on the rent for his mistress. She was just leaving as I pulled on to her street, so I followed her discreetly as she turned and headed south toward the highway.

Eventually, her convertible Mercedes pulled into one of her favourite destinations according to Pooley's report, the Northpark Mall. I parked a few rows away and watched her as she crossed the lot.

Monique was beautiful, more than what I expected from the pictures Pooley had taken. She had natural beauty, high cheekbones on an unblemished face. Her hair was blond and stylish, not piled high like most of the Texas women heading across the parking lot. She wore baggy clothes over what must have been an athletic figure.

I followed her inside, trailing furtively. She crossed through the department store, Neiman Marcus, and headed into the mall proper. I waited while she window-shopped, using the glass of the storefronts across the corridor to watch her as she disappeared inside a Pottery Barn.

I waited for her to come out, but when she didn't, I made my way over to the store as casually as possible, face blank, hands deep in my pockets.

I could hear shouting from outside the store, but the voices grew clearer as I moved closer. Monique was standing at the sales counter, her face contorted in rage, screaming obscenities at two clerks on the other side of the table. Her face had transformed; where I had seen beauty before, now I saw raw ugliness. The dispute had something to do with a promised item not being in stock, and the poor clerks were cowering from this woman, this privileged woman, this mistress, who was lording over them, raging over them, simply because she could.

She would not be raging for long.

I watched her across the parking lot with narrowed eyes, allowing my hatred for this woman to build. Pooley had mentioned a 'difficult' personality in the file, but I had a special enmity for those who treat others like shit. The mark of character is how we treat people who can do nothing for us – the secretaries, the waitresses, the bank tellers, the check-out lady at the grocery store. She was making this job easier.

I followed her to a medical building and waited in the parking lot while she met with her doctor. Whatever illness she was attempting to cure would cease to matter as soon as she returned to her apartment.

She didn't have any other errands and so headed for home in Deep Ellum. I sat in my car for a good hour after she entered the building.

Most professional assassinations take place in the target's home. It is important for an assassin to let his prey settle into a routine, to get comfortable, to drop his or her guard in the familiar surroundings of where he or she lives.

I checked the clip on my Glock and headed inside, then took the elevator up to the fourth floor.

Her door had a standard Fleer lock. It took me less than ten seconds to pick it and quietly crack the door. Quickly, I entered the apartment, ready to strike if need be, but she wasn't in the living room or the kitchen off to the side. I heard the unmistakable sound of a shower faucet being turned in the master bedroom and moved in that direction.

Silently, I turned the bedroom door handle and pushed the door in at the same time. I took a step forward and only had a second to duck my head as a golf club swung my way. I managed to avoid a direct hit from the club head as she only grazed my skull with the graphite shaft. Still, I had to fight off the surprise of being discovered in the act, and I wasn't ready for the intensity of this woman.

She whipped the club back and prepared to strike a second time. She was only half dressed, and something about her bare legs caused me a moment's hesitation, which she took advantage of, swinging the club low and connecting with my left shin. I felt the bone crack and a flash of stars blurred my vision, but instincts took over and reminded me that whatever this woman was, she wasn't an experienced killer.

She tried to pass me, to get out of the bedroom to the more advantageous battlefield of the living room, and she almost made it, but I lunged for her and caught her arm, twisted her wrist back and jerked her body to the floor.

From there, it was a scrum. I had a hundred pound advantage, and although she had the desperation of a cornered rat, I used the pain in my shin to focus my intensity. I clawed at those bare legs until I was able to get on top of her. She tried to scratch me, to bite me, her jaws snapping like a turtle's, her eyes wild, rolling in their sockets. She pounded the heel of her foot into my shin, but I was focused, feeding on the pain, and I managed to pin her arms down, straddling her torso while I hooked my fingers around her throat.

I was getting ready to finish the job when I heard Monique's front door open behind me.

Fuck. I had to make a decision, had to time it right. While Monique struggled under my grip, I concentrated my hearing, listening for the telltale sound of footsteps approaching the door to the bedroom. Even with my bum leg, I could hoist myself backward off of her and use surprise and a solid forearm to get the new visitor down on the ground. From there, I would have to hope I had sapped the fight out of this woman so she wouldn't be able to help.

'Columbus!'

The last thing I was expecting was Pooley's voice coming from the living room.

'Columbus!'

Even as I processed this, I could feel my fingers loosening on Monique's throat. She coughed and made her body go as limp as a possum's.

Pooley appeared in the light of the living room, drawn by the coughing. He was sweating and breathing hard, and he peered in at me in the bedroom as I slid off the woman.

'She . . . uh . . .' he was trying to catch his breath. 'She's not the target.'

'What?'

As soon as I lifted my body off Monique's torso, she scrambled backward to the corner of the bedroom, leaving her back against the wall, hugging her knees and sobbing between coughing spasms.

'I fucked up. I . . . uh . . . the double fee . . . the two names . . . I thought it was . . .'

'This isn't . . .'

'She's pregnant. The hit is on the baby inside her.'

'Fuck.'

I stood up and Monique screamed, flinching back, her hands on her stomach.

I put my palms up in a calming motion, but I was

staring hotly at Pooley. 'Fuck,' I repeated. 'How do you make that mistake?'

'I didn't catch it . . . I should have but I didn't. That's why I got here as soon as I could.'

I turned my eyes on Monique and she flinched.

'I'm leaving,' I said to her. 'I'm not going to kill you or your baby. But someone put a professional hit on that child and didn't care enough to explain it wasn't on you.'

She nodded, but her mouth was still pulled back in a snarl, like she was ready to fight again if I made a move in her direction.

I limped out of her apartment and Pooley helped me down the stairs all the way to his car.

What kind of person would put a hit on the child when hitting the mother would have served the same purpose? And what kind of psychological game was the person playing to sign off on the kill that way . . . name the unborn daughter but present it like it was the mother? Was it so the man or woman could rest easier knowing the assassination was little more than a forced abortion? So the person could blame the mother's death on the shooter, since it wasn't in the contract? The sin of omission easier to stomach than the sin of execution? Maybe I didn't want to know the answer. But I didn't finish the job that day, didn't go through with the assassination, because I didn't like being manipulated.

★   ★   ★

In Portland, the sky is cloudless for the first time in weeks and it feels as though someone has lifted a blanket. The horizon is clear, endless.

Abe Mann is heading to Sacramento, his last stop before heading to a convention in Los Angeles he will never reach. I am watching a news clip about Sacramento and Mann's impending arrival on the *Today Show* as I brush my teeth in the hotel mirror and a name starts to tickle the back of my mind like it is trying to get my attention.

Skyline Hall.

Skyline Hall in Sacramento.

When on a job, assassins sometimes pepper their conversations with nuggets from their real lives, their real backgrounds, to add sincerity, a touch of authenticity to whatever cover they're using to get in close to a target. This tactic has its strengths, usually gaining a mark's confidence to be exploited. But this tactic also has its shortcomings, like when it is employed on someone who isn't a target at the time, someone who remembers, someone who might become an enemy.

Skyline Hall in Sacramento.

Hap Blowenfeld told me a story the first time I met him as we loaded beer crates into the back of his truck, a story so I would bond with him, a story about how he had killed a kid with his bare hands over the theft of his father's wallet and had been sent to Skyline Hall in Sacramento, California, a Juvey centre like Waxham.

If this story is true, if Hap had been at that Juvey centre, then there might be some record of what his real name is, of where his father lives, of a living relative, of a way to get to him.

# Chapter Fifteen

There are two ways to get information you aren't supposed to have. One is to sneak in and steal it. The other is to force someone to give it to you.

Skyline Hall for Boys is on the outskirts of Sacramento, on a deserted stretch of highway, away from any major roads. It looks like a high school with razor wire, a place built a long time ago with zero funding for repairs.

I case it for a day and mark the shift changes. Like with Richard Levine's security force, I know the best time to strike will be when the front desk is at its most chaotic, when tired government employees are handing the keys to the asylum over to bored government employees just getting started on another shitty day in juvenile hell.

I head up to the front doors and make my way to a chubby receptionist who is literally watching the clock.

'May I help you?' she asks without shifting her eyes to me.

'Yes. Hi. I'm with State Senator Vespucci's office. Can you point me to the records room?'

Now her eyes move from the clock to examine my face. She is pissed. I have arrived looking like work at the end of a long shift. Her face tightens until her mouth disappears into a thin line.

'What's this regarding?'

'It's pertaining research for funding grants.'

'No one told me.'

'Well, there was a fax sent a few days ago.'

She casts her eyes to an empty back office where an old fax machine sits on a shelf, then back at me, trying to decide if she wants to heave her considerable bulk out of her desk chair with only ten minutes left in her shift.

Finally, she sighs and gets up.

She moves inside the office and heads to the fax machine, looks around for some stray papers, but doesn't find any.

'Well, listen here. I don't know anything about no . . .'

She stops in the middle of her sentence, because I have come up behind her silently and now stand with a gun pressed against her rib cage. Outside that office, there is a little commotion as the new shift of workers enters, but inside, where we are, it is quiet.

Under her breath, she manages, 'Oh, lordy . . .'

'What's your name?'

She whispers, 'Roberta.'

'Roberta, you have a decision to make. We live in a world where we have choices and for good or bad, there are consequences to those choices. Now you're going to have to make one.'

'Don't Mister . . .'

'Choice one is you do exactly what I tell you to do and no one in this building dies. Not Lawrence the janitor, not Bill the counselling rep, not you, Roberta. And not those cute little grandkids whose pictures I saw taped to your desk.'

'Oh, lordy . . .'

'Choice two is you raise your voice, you cause a stink, you draw attention to me or yourself, and I go on a killing spree the likes of which Sacramento has never seen. Nod your head if you understand.'

She nods her head, her eyes never leaving mine, her face red, stinging, like someone slapped her across the cheeks.

'Good. Then no one is going to get shot today.'

I lower the gun so she'll know she's given the right answer, made progress.

'Okay, Roberta, now you're going to lead me to the records room. When we're in there, you're going to point me to the files covering the five-year period from 1984 to 1989. Can you do that for me, Roberta?'

She nods again, and then mechanically, robotically, she leads me out of the office and down a side corridor. No one looks at us, no one greets us, no one asks us what we're doing. It's just another Tuesday in a place where no one cares.

We spend just over an hour in the records room, undisturbed. Roberta has dropped her guard and is helping me dig through the materials, showing me booking photos of each child. Thankfully, they've been catalogued by offences, so I narrow the field to the most serious felonies, and I can skip over all the faces except the white ones, which makes the task even quicker. Still, there was an abundance of teenagers committing felonies back in the heyday of West Coast gang violence, so the job is still arduous.

Just when my patience is wearing thin and I think maybe Hap got the details right but changed the geography, I find the right picture staring back at me.

Younger, with more hair and less confidence, a teen-age Hap Blowenfeld glares out from a black and white photograph with an expression of faux defiance. The name on the file is Evan Feldman. It has an address for his father in Arcadia. It seems the only detail Hap changed was his name, and even that isn't too far of a stretch.

'That's it, then?' asks Roberta.

'That's it.'

'You gonna let me go, now?'

'How old are your grandkids, Roberta?'

Her eyes flash a little, like she has gotten comfortable with me and now regrets it. Softly, she whispers, 'The boy is five. The girl, three.'

'Well, if you want the boy to see six and the girl to see four, you forget you ever saw me and you don't mention this to anyone.'

'No, sir, I wouldn't.'

'If you do, some men might try to arrest me, but they won't. Some others might try to kill me, but they won't. And I'll know it was you who told someone about today, Roberta. And then I'll come back to Sacramento. And let me tell you something as sure as I'm standing before you, I don't want to come back to Sacramento.'

'You won't have no reason to.' A tear spills down her cheek but her voice doesn't crack.

'I know I won't. I'm gonna take this.'

I pick up Hap's juvenile file and head out the door. I'm sure it will be a long time before Roberta gathers the strength to leave the room.


Arcadia is a town of urban sprawl gone wrong. It's buildings, buildings, buildings and concrete and asphalt and sewers and shit as far as the eye can see, all surrounding a horse track improperly named after a Saint, all within a stone's throw of the bad side of Los Angeles.

The address I have is on a residential street lined with squat one-storey houses packed as close together as the city planners will allow. None of the houses seem too eager to do battle with an earthquake, should a fresh one arrive.

The address I have for Hap's father, Tom Feldman, is 416 N. Armstrong Rd., and as I scope out the unassuming house from down the street, I find myself praying there's an older white man still living in it. Just don't be a dead end. Not when I feel like I'm so fucking close.

There are times in life when Fate smiles on you, when you ask for a piece of luck and that piece arrives in a box with a bow on it. I asked for luck when I killed that prostitute back in Pennsylvania, what the fuck was her name, I can't even remember it now, just the smell of that grape bubble gum in the passenger seat of my rental car, and I was asking for luck here, luck I had done my homework, I had guessed right, Hap's old man hadn't died or moved or been kicked out for not making his mortgage payments. And here's the thing: luck has a way of shining on preparation, of rewarding those who put themselves in a position to take advantage of it when that gift box with the pretty bow plops into their laps.

Hap's father parks his car in his driveway, gets out and heads to his mailbox. His face unmistakably belongs to the sire of the man who killed my partner;

father and son share the same features, the same small nose, the same eyes. I can feel anger and excitement building up inside me.

I slam my door shut and hurry down the street.

'Sir . . . ?'

He looks up innocently. 'Yes?'

'Are you Tom Feldman?'

'Yes . . .'

'Thank God . . . How you doing?'

'Fine . . . ?' It is more of a question than a statement.

'I'm so glad I found you. I'm friends with Evan . . .'

A broad smile crosses his face . . . 'Really? Well, nice to meet you . . .'

'Jack . . .'

'Nice to meet you, Jack. Evan should be here any minute.'

My heart leaps up into my throat. He's coming *here?* I haven't just found the father; I've got the son, right here, right now. The gift box just got shinier. The bow a little bigger.

But I need the element of surprise and if Hap or Evan or whatever the fuck his name is drives up now, the tables could turn in a matter of seconds. I manage to say, 'Excellent! He'll be so happy to see me.'

His dad pulls out a cell phone. 'He probably stopped off to load up on groceries. Let me call him and tell him you're here, Jack. Hurry him on his way.'

I keep my voice even, keep the smile on my face . . . 'That'd be great.' I pause, like I'm thinking more about it. 'You know what, though? He has no idea I'm coming to see him and I'd love to surprise him.'

His dad laughs. 'Sure. He hasn't kept up with any of his old friends, so this'll be a nice treat for him.'

I look down the street, my ears straining to pick up the sound of an approaching engine. I need to get out of the front yard, be inside the house when Hap comes through the door with grocery bags in his hands.

'Can I use your bathroom?'

'Of course.'

He leads the way up his front steps. 'How do you know Evan?'

'We used to run trucks together in Boston. Ten years ago.'

'You're kidding me. Well, I'll be.'

He approaches the front door, and my instincts fail me, I don't see it coming, I am so sure Fate is smiling on me that I don't notice the warning signs. The father asking to use his cell phone. The quick way he warmed to me.

We reach the front door and the old man opens it in a flourish and screams . . . 'Evan! There's a killer here . . .' and then I bash him in the side of the head before he can say any more but it's already too late.

I counted on a lot of things but one thing I never imagined is Hap telling his old man exactly what he did for a living. I didn't count on Hap being home and I didn't count on his father covering for him, and I didn't count on that old bastard bellowing out like a wailing siren.

I barely see a flash of feet bounding up a nearby staircase before I have a chance to get my bearings, have my eyes adjust to the light. If he had cared about his father before, enough to throttle a kid who had stolen his old man's wallet, he certainly doesn't care any more. The years of being a bag man have forced the survival instinct into him, and he is fleeing. If I kill his father, so be it.

I sprint into the house and dart for the stairwell when a volley of bullets cascade down at me like a dozen wasps defending the nest. As soon as the avalanche recedes and I hear his feet clomping away, I fire through the ceiling and then hurry up the steps two at a time.

I peek around the corner quickly, just enough to catch a glimpse, fully expecting another shot, but instead, I see Hap smash through a second-storey window and I am moving to the end of the hallway and looking down and he is already rolling up off the grass like a cat and running away. I don't hesitate and fling myself out the window, bracing my knees to absorb the fall, and then roll with it and up at the same time.

He should have been waiting for me to jump and then shot me as soon as I hit the ground but he didn't and I'm up and running after him without missing a step. I'm faster than he is, and he's going to have to make a move as we sprint across lawn after lawn, but I can tell something is wrong with him, something's amiss. He hasn't tried to pop a shot off at me since the spray of bullets down the stairwell, hasn't tried to distract me or keep me at bay so he can duck between houses, and I realize I'm in luck after all; I caught Hap unprepared. He had to scramble off his father's couch when the old man signalled him and he only had time to sprint up the stairs and grab his gun but he had been lazy and hadn't scooped up a second clip and he's out of bullets now.

He makes his move, and just as a young couple down the street steps out of their front door, Hap lowers his shoulder and barrels into the house. I am twenty steps behind him and the husband just looks at me and yells 'hey!' but he sees my gun out and grabs his wife and backs away and I am past him and through the front door and I am hoping the layout of this house is different from Hap's father's house, different than the house he grew up in, but it looks familiar, and I hear a clinking coming from a nearby doorway, a drawer overturning in the kitchen and I scramble to the sound and smash through the swinging door but he is on me before I can get into the room and he buries a knife into my shoulder.

'Hiya, Columbus!' he says with eyes filled to the brim with fire.

I fall and my gun clatters across the tile floor in the kitchen and Hap scrambles for it, but I trip him up with my good arm and he topples and I am smashing him in the ribs with my fist as hard as I can.

Ten minutes is all we have to kill each other. Ten minutes from when that young husband whipped out his cell phone and dialled 9-1-1 as soon as we blitzed by him into his house, so if we're gonna do this, we need to do it now and get it finished and get the fuck out of here. Hap knows it and I know it and we're going to fight right here to the death in this middle-class suburban kitchen because there's no time and no other way to do it and it is and might as well be. He drives his fist into the kitchen knife handle buried in my shoulder, and fuck if I'm not blacking out but this is a goddamn hand-to-hand fight to the death and I cannot afford to go dark. Not now. Not after all I've done, not after I travelled from East to West, from Spring to Winter, from present to past to present and saw so much and gave up so much. Not now when the finish line is so close I can smell it like the salt in the air.

I open my jaws as wide as I can and bite into his side like a rabid dog and his arm that was reaching for my gun on the tile floor is forced back involuntarily by the pain and that's all I need. I get my knees under me and leap for the gun past his retreating arm and I snatch it up in my good hand, my left hand, and flip over and point it at Hap's head with my finger on the trigger, and I see it in his eyes. The life goes out of them like the electricity has been cut. He is defeated.

'Fuck.'

'Yeah.'

'Vespucci fingered me?'

'No. He stayed true blue.'

'Then how?'

'You told me a story once. The first time I loaded truck for you.'

'What?'

'You told me you killed a man who stole your father's wallet. You told me you did time at Skyline Hall in Sacramento.'

He nods now, resigned. 'I did?'

'Yeah.'

'I was still pretty new at this then.'

'Yeah.'

'Look, I'm sorry I killed your man. I was just doing what you would have done.'

'Yeah.'

He tries to sit up straighter, but the pain from my bite makes him wince a bit. 'Then I guess you gotta do what you gotta . . .'

I shoot Hap in the head at close range and his face disappears before he can finish the sentence.

Five minutes now. With a bloody arm, with a knife stuck in my shoulder, but with something else too: resolve. I climb to my feet, open the kitchen door that leads directly to the back yard and I am moving through it, into the sunlight, blinking my eyes.

# Chapter Sixteen

I am the son.

The same side, the same shoulder, the same fucking arm. First a bullet, then a knife, and now my arm is virtually useless. It has turned an ugly shade of black – even against my skin it is prominent – and I'm not sure if it will ever function properly. I have it cleaned and bandaged and I hit myself with a cocktail of medications but I'm not a triage doctor and if I tried to seek professional help now I'd be out of the game.

There's a dead man named Evan Feldman in his neighbour's kitchen and there's my blood splashed on that floor and they'll be looking for a wounded man with blood type B positive trying to get stitched up at emergency rooms all over the city. I'm stuck with one worthless arm and the convention is now two days away and I have seventeen hours until

Congressman Abe Mann will be alone on the twenty-second floor of the Standard Hotel in downtown Los Angeles.

I am the son.

Pooley is dead and the man who killed him is dead and Mr Cox is dead and so many others are dead and Vespucci is alive and full of regrets. I am alive, but I'm not whole.

I have seventeen hours and I'll be damned if I am defeated now. Not after all this, not after I let the past back in and it forced me to my knees and goddammit, GOD DAMN IT, I'm losing my grip on the slippery ball of sanity floating somewhere in my head. There's a mirror in this cheap hotel room where the clerk didn't even look up when he took my cash and handed me a key, and my face is gaunt and pained and stretched as tight as a guitar string. I look into my own eyes and I force them to stare back at me, force them to fill up with that same resolve I've always relied upon, that same resolve that improbably got me out of that bedroom in Italy, that same resolve that kicked Jake Owens in the stomach in her apartment in Boston. I am Columbus, a Silver Bear, and whoever hired three assassins to kill Abe Mann the week of his nomination will not be disappointed because I am the son.

So how to get close to a man who has more security surrounding him than almost any man on Earth? How to get close to him even though I'm out of time and wounded and I have no resources at my finger-tips?

And then it comes to me. The only solution, the only way to finish this. It was in front of me the whole time; it was in Vespucci's words and in my own mantra and it is as clear to me as the sky after a storm.

I fashion a sling out of a white T-shirt and shower and make myself as presentable as possible. In the dust-caked mirror, I shave my face and check my reflection and nod, pleased. I look plain and unas-suming. The injury is unfortunate, a red flag, but nevertheless I no longer look like an escaped mental patient.

I drive from the decrepit hotel on the outskirts of East Los Angeles to Interstate 10 and then off a few side streets to Grant and the front of the Standard. The hotel is modern and angular and stark in that West Coast style that emphasizes design flair over comfort. A valet parker exchanges a ticket for my keys and I enter the white lobby and get my bearings.

It doesn't take me long to find what I'm seeking. A coterie of secret service agents huddle near a bank of elevators, stern expressions on their faces, eyes hid-den behind dark sunglasses. A blonde female whom I recognize from standing on the sides of daises in Indianapolis and Seattle is dressed differently from the security officers but shares their grave expres-sions. She is holding a clipboard.

I approach her and feel every eye shift toward me, sizing up my arm in the makeshift sling.

'Excuse me.'

'Yes?' She studies me with a smile that looks as though it were forced on to her face under duress.

'How would I go about seeing Congressman Mann?'

She snorts and I see two of the Secret Service officers move their hands inside their jackets.

'I'm sorry. The congressman is unavailable at the moment.'

'He'll see me.'

She looks at the agents and they nod as if to tell her they are ready for any move I might make.

'And you are?'

'I'm his son . . .' and immediately they have me under the arm and are leading me forcefully away.

'Tell him LaWanda Dickerson's son! Tell him that!'

She looks at me queerly as I am jerked into an empty conference room off the lobby. Ten secret service officers materialize like magic and follow me into the room.

The senior officer is a man of forty or so with a bald head and hard eyes. He speaks with a higher voice than I would have guessed, like air blowing through an organ pipe, but he also speaks calmly, soothingly.

'Okay, friend. Let's start by seeing some identification. Can you hand me your wallet?'

I shake my head. 'I don't have one.'

'No identification?'

'No.'

'What's your name?'

'John Smith.'

He smiles, showing me I'm not going to get under his skin. 'Okay, John. I'm going to have the man behind you pat you down while I keep a gun pointed at your head. Is that okay?'

'Yes.'

This tells him two things. One, I'm not carrying a gun or a knife because he knows a man who is about to be patted down would gain nothing by lying about it. And two, I don't fear having a gun on me, which means I've undoubtedly had experience with it before. I can see this work itself out in his mind, but he keeps his face even. He pulls out his pistol and does as he said he'd do, points it a mere foot from my forehead.

'Are you carrying a bomb?'

All the eyes in the room are riveted on me.

'No.'

'What's wrong with your arm, John?'

'I was shot and then I was stabbed.'

'You sound like a busy man.'

'Yes.'

'Okay, John. Stand up and Larry will frisk you now.'

231

'Go easy on the arm.'

'Okay, John.'

I rise to my feet and the large man behind me pats me down as thoroughly as if he's taking my measurements. I wince as he searches up my bandaged arm and under it, not going easy at all. I regret saying anything; naturally that's where he'd search the hardest for anything untoward.

Larry nods at the senior officer and he lowers his gun. 'Okay, John. You are unarmed. You may sit.'

'Thank you.'

'What is your business with Congressman Mann?'

'That's between Congressman Mann and myself.'

'Okay, John. Would you mind if we took your fingerprints?'

'I don't mind.'

'Great.'

A pad of ink is produced and I get my fingers ready but before they are pressed onto the moist purple pad a door opens and a female voice speaks up to a room as silent as a graveyard. 'Abe wants to see him.'

The blonde with the clipboard. She chews the inside of her cheek, anxious.

The senior agent doesn't hesitate. 'That's a negative.'

'Abe insists.'

'Negative.'

'Would you like to speak to him, Steve? Because he certainly isn't listening to me.'

Steve nods and moves to a corner of the room, pulls out a cell phone and speaks softly. I can tell he's arguing with my father on the other end of the line, and I wait and it soon becomes clear he is losing the argument. His face falls but then he looks at me and his eyes harden again. I can make out that he says 'yes' into the phone before flipping the lid closed.

Twelve secret service officers lead me down a hall-way with Larry on my left and Steve on my right and we are moving like a hangman's caravan toward two doors at the end of the corridor, the big suite on the top floor. We reach the doors and Steve gives me a curt 'wait here' and he enters into the room alone.

I wait for ten minutes, keeping my body neutral the way I've practised for the last ten years until the doors open again and Steve emerges.

'Now, listen, John. There are going to be ground rules and if you deviate from those rules, we will not hesitate to kill you.'

I wait.

'You will enter the room and stand behind the line I've drawn for you on the floor. If you step over that line, Congressman Mann will ring a buzzer he's holding which will vibrate in my hand and I will enter the door and shoot you dead. Do you believe me?'

'I do.'

'You have ten minutes to walk out of that door. If you are still in the room after ten minutes I will enter and I will shoot you dead. Do you believe this to be true?'

'I do.'

'Okay, John. Then I'm going to let you in the room and start the clock. Please don't raise your voice. It might make all of us a little antsy and I don't want us to be antsy, okay?'

'Yes.'

'All right then.'

Steve opens the door and I step inside the suite.

A small foyer leads to a spacious living room. A red line of tape marks off the two rooms and I enter and put my toes on the line and there he is, after all this way, there he is sitting on a grey sofa thirty feet away, his eyes fixed on me like they are attached by a rope. He is bigger up close than he looked on all those stages and there isn't an ounce of apprehension on his face.

'Hello. I'm Abe.'

'My name is Columbus. And I am your son.'

I say this as calmly as if I were announcing the weather.

'How do you figure, Columbus?'

'I was the baby inside LaWanda Dickerson whom you knew as Amanda B. when you had her killed your freshman year in the Congress.'

He does not look down nor away. He is very good at holding his gaze steady, a conditioned skill that has served him well.

'It wasn't like that, son. I needed her to leave Washington and some men who were looking out for me took their job too seriously, too far.'

He stands up, keeping his hands in his pockets. 'But how do you know I'm the father?'

'I know.'

'She was a professional prostitute . . .'

'I know.' I'm answering his first question.

He looks at me the way an architect looks over his final blueprints, searching for flaws, mistakes. But he finds none.

'I do too. I can tell just by looking at you.' He exhales, heavily. 'But why come now? What do you want?'

'I was hired to kill you.'

He swallows once and removes his hand from his pocket. He's holding a silver box with a button on it. 'To kill me?'

'Yes, I'm a professional killer. I've killed men and women all over the world. I do this because I was born to do it. Do you understand?'

'Yes.' He looks at his hand and back at me. 'Let me ask you something. Do you think it was a coincidence you of all people were hired to kill me?'

'Someone told me fate has a way of making paths cross.'

'Yes. We just move through this world like so many puppets on strings.'

'No. Not me. I'm in control. Our paths crossed because I willed myself to get here.'

He studies me, like he's mulling this over.

'Do you think you were lucky? To get up into this room?'

'I think luck often favours the artful.'

'So how are you going to do it?'

'I'm going to improvise.'

'Before I press this button?'

'Yes.'

He nods matter-of-factly, then takes his thumb off the button and places the silver box on the glass coffee table.

'How are you going to escape?'

'I don't know.'

'That's not much of a plan.'

'No. But I got this far.'

'Yes, you did.'

'You have no idea what it took me to get here.'

'I presume your whole life, all your struggles, led to this moment.'

'Yes.'

'How much time do you have?'

'Six minutes.'

'Then listen to me. Here's how you're going to escape. You kill me and then you move through that door which leads to the master bedroom. The window is open and there are balconies going down. But there is also a balcony going up to the roof. You climb to the roof and you will find a window-washing cart on the opposite side of the building. Use the gearshift to drop at a rapid speed twenty floors to the alley below. You can be several blocks away before Officer Steve comes through that door.'

I've kept a poker face during this speech but I don't understand, can't comprehend what he's saying. 'Why are you telling me this?'

'Because I hired you.'

The truth rings out in the empty hotel room like a strong wind sweeping in and carrying out the fog.

'But why?'

'Like I said, I'm just a puppet on a string.'

'That's not good enough.'

'You only have four minutes, son. It's going to have to be good enough if you want to live.'

'But that's just it. *You* don't want to live.'

'You think I have a choice? I'm a bad person, son. I'm bad in a thousand ways. There is only one way out of this . . . I've tried everything else. I don't call the shots. I can't even scandal my way off the train. I'm not that man on television. I'm a monster.'

'Explain.'

He sits down heavily, like this confession has sapped his final bit of energy. 'Three minutes,' he says, weakly.

'Explain.' I repeat through gritted teeth.

237

'I didn't kill your mother. I didn't know they were going to do . . . *that*. Politics . . . politicians . . . we don't vote, we don't make decisions, hell, we don't even put on our own goddam shoes without someone telling us exactly what to do. Don't you see? Too many people rely on us to feed the machine, too many people own every little part of us to let vice tether us down. Power isn't in the big rooms in the Capitol, it's in the shadows and the corners and the dirty space under the rug.'

He's gaining momentum, picking up his natural cadence, speaking like he did in Portland, speaking like he did when he actually believed what he was saying.

'When I had my *problem* with your mother, some dark men made that problem disappear. You understand about dark men, I take it. I wouldn't have dreamed that . . .'

'And Nichelle Spellman in Kansas City? And how many others?'

He lowers his eyes. 'I can't stop it. It's like a black hole's been pulling me in all these years. There's no escape. Not for me. There are corrupt people who run this country. Really run it. Their interests are motivated by greed, by money. They'll do whatever they have to do to prop me up, keep me in power. They'll carve me in pieces till there's nothing left but scraps for the vultures.'

His speech is gravelly now, shaken, like the words themselves have been beaten down, pummelled, and his eyes are blank, as though he's talking to himself. 'And what do you think's going to happen after? When I win? What do you think's going to happen when I control policy, when I'm in charge of the NSA, when I'm Commander in Chief of the whole god-damn military? You think these dark men are going to vanish? You think they're going to let me be?

'Or do you think they're going to be emboldened, inspirited, galvanized to push the blackness further? I can't . . .' He shakes his head. 'I can't stop them. They won't let me stop them. My only choice is to . . . escape.'

I keep my voice filled with ice. 'You could cast them off. Force your own way.'

'No. You don't understand.'

'Buck them off your back, throw a chair through a window, escape . . .'

'No.'

'You could try. And if they hit you, rest and try again.'

'Maybe a long time ago. I'm tired now.'

'You could stay in the present, fight off the past, become a new man . . .'

'Impossible.'

'*You* can control your future. *You* can bend it to your will.'

'I can't.'

'You're a coward.'

'Yes.'

I look at the man before me, and he looks smaller than he did when I first entered the room. I have just one more question. 'Did you know? Did you know I'd be the one coming for you?'

He searches my face through half-closed lids. 'Would it help you if I said I did?'

I cross the room and am on him before he can take another breath. My fingers are on his throat and I squeeze with my left hand, my right hand useless, and our faces are inches apart but he has shut his eyes, letting this happen, and he doesn't resist, doesn't flinch as I close my fingers around his windpipe and then tear the skin and rip the throat out by sheer force, a grip more powerful than I can imagine, and Cox and Pooley and Dan Levine and Janet Stephens and Hap recede into the shadows, fade away, and blood is spraying that grey couch like a geyser emptying its crystal clear water and Abe Mann's eyes shoot open and roll back and he gags on his own blood, slumping off the couch and rolling on to the floor.

I am up and through the bedroom door and the window is open and I know he wasn't lying, maybe for the first time in a long time, he wasn't lying, and the words he said to me about my escape were honest and right and true.

I climb the balcony and scale the final eight feet to the roof and sprint across the gravel and tar to the other side like a man being granted his freedom and it's right there as he said it would be, an empty window-washer's cart like a boat across Styx, and I hit the button and it lowers quickly. My shoulder aches but I ignore it and the wind picks up and blows hard into my face and I can taste a bit of salt in the air from the endless ocean to the west.

# Epilogue

I step out of the white Mercedes van and the driver opens my door and hands me my suitcase. The hotel is as I remember it, built into the side of the hill like a natural addition to the landscape. My room is large and comfortable and I walk to the patio overlooking the town and the sea far below and I cast my eyes up the hill and across until they settle on the Cortino house.

I wonder who lives in it now. It has been six years since the bodies of Cortino, his invalid wife, and his bodyguard were found murdered in their bedroom on an early June morning. The crime slapped the sleepy town awake, sent it reeling, but the passage of time and the endless lapping of the ocean on its doorstep gently nudged the town back to sleep. I imagine the doors of the houses high up on the hill are locked at night now.

The city of Los Angeles had a similar reaction the second time a nominee was assassinated while in its care. But there was no Sirhan Sirhan to exact revenge upon, just a John Smith with a nondescript face and a pleasant voice and an ability to vanish into thin air. Two years later, the case remains unsolved, despite every effort to gain some answers.

I am here in Positano getting my mind right. It is late summer and I informed Mr Ryan I would need a few months between assignments this time. A few months without making connections, without severing connections, just a few months to breathe and live and remember.

I have worked exclusively in Europe since the Abe Mann killing, and Mr Ryan moved to Paris to facilitate his role in my work. He has found the move from the desert to be agreeable, the law enforcement here more relaxed, the economy strong, the supply of contracts endless. I believe he is happy having a Silver Bear under his aegis, though we don't talk about personal things. Ours is a business relationship, and things are simple.

He travelled recently to Denver, Colorado upon my request. It is the first time he has made a file on a person who wasn't a target. I have the file in my hand now, but I haven't opened it. I was waiting until I arrived in this place, this town built into the side of a hill yearning to tumble into the sea. I sit heavily on a patio chair, breathe in the cool night air, and place my thumb under the seal.

The name at the top of the page is Jacqueline Grant, formerly Jake Owens of Boston, Massachusetts. The surveillance photo shows a profile of a woman stepping out of a car, hurrying across a parking lot to a grocery store. Her hair is longer than it was when I knew her and her face is a bit fuller. She looks content, or maybe I'm projecting this on to her image.

She has been married for three years. Her husband owns a restaurant. A clean, well-lighted place that serves hamburgers to locals. He is her age and treats her well. I wonder how they met. I wonder if she was unlucky with men after I kicked her in the stomach or if she swore them off until Alex Grant came into her life. I wonder if he was safe and she felt secure with him.

I wonder if she loves him.